Ruffled Feathers

by

Jason Blacker

PUBLISHED BY:
Lemon Tree Publishing
Copyright © 2013
Jason Blacker

Visit www.JasonBlacker.com on the web to stay up to date

Editing: Andrea Anesi

ISBN: 9781927623381

For Angela and Kraigh – I soar high upon your wings

Table of Contents

Squire's Spoon

"Do you understand the severity of the charges against you?" asked Mr. Crow.

Mr. Mallard sat perched in the large, gnarled oak tree that was Mr. Crow's office of sorts. Mallard couldn't understand what the fuss was about. More than that, he was concerned about his lawyer. Mr. Crow had a great reputation, but looking around his office, you wouldn't believe it.

Papers of all sorts, scraps really, were tossed higgledy-piggledy about, and Mr. Crow pecked through them, grumbling to himself, trying to find the one he was looking for. Mallard watched Crow look around for awhile until he finally gave up.

"It's not important right now anyway," Mr.

Crow said. "Tomorrow we go to trial Mr. Mallard and this is very serious indeed."

Mallard couldn't help but smile to himself. He thought the whole thing was quite bizarre and wonderfully entertaining. But Mr. Crow had furrowed brows and was in no mood for frivolity. He looked wise with his monocle and old with his gray eyebrows and sideburns.

"Really, Mr. Mallard, at the very least you must try and act contrite. The Parliament is headed by Tyto Alba who will be the presiding judge. His consulting judges are Asio Otus and Bubo Africanis. These are not men to be toyed with. They take a very serious stand on this sort of behavior. They are also known for meting out the harshest of punishments if the accused is not seen as contrite."

"Can I go back and splash in the water? It looks oh so inviting," asked Mallard as he looked down at the big lake filled like a blanket with his friends.

"Mr. Mallard!"

Crow was upset and his old voice cracked under the strain as he tried his sternest tone on Mr. Mallard.

"Have you not been listening to a word I've said? This may not be punishable by death but it certainly is the next thing to it. It might as well be a death sentence if you're found guilty. And with Mr. Alba at the helm, any, and I mean any, acting out on your behalf is not going to help. He'll slam that gavel down with the resounding echo of guilty."

"But they say you're the best," replied Mallard.

"I am only as good as my client is willing to allow."

Crow started looking around for that darned paper again.

"I really must find it," he muttered to himself.

"I can help you if you'd like," said Mallard. "What are you looking for?"

Mr. Crow raised a gray bushy eyebrow at the young man sitting in his office.

"I can find it myself. I'd rather you not see it until I've found it and showed it to you."

Crow wobbled around his office, his fine black suite a little gray for wear and age. His regal head bobbing up and down as he walked this way and that across his office, looking under this pile and then under that. Mallard gazed down at the pond and wondered when he'd be able to go for a dip again with his friends. He dreamed of diving and splashing in the cool water, his feathers slick with the wet embrace of it all. It was just so unfair that everyone had gotten their knickers in a knot over such a trivial thing. And to think that they were taking it all so seriously was beyond him.

"Aha, here it is!" exclaimed Mr. Crow. "Now this is what I wanted to show you. I hate to do it, but you just don't seem to understand the severity of the trouble you're in."

Crow came back over to where Mallard was sitting and put the picture in front of him. Mallard looked at the image and gasped. He was horrified, he couldn't believe in such things, such cruelty and barbarism. Not at the hands of his own people. If he were alone he would have cried. He knew that for certain. But sitting here next to the wise and old, and perhaps discombobulated but apparently erudite, Mr. Crow he dared not. He didn't think the old man would understand.

"That's awful, horrible and mean," said Mallard, looking away as he felt sick to his stomach.

"I know, son, I know. But this is the severity of the charges brought against you. You see what they did to this poor chap, Cygnus Atratus. Look at those fine wings, mangled and clipped to almost nothing. I have to show you one more thing."

Crow reached behind his back and brought out another picture. This one was of the very same Mr. Atratus. His matte black suit dabbled and streaked with red. Mallard couldn't look at it. He couldn't hold back the sadness in his soul. He burst into tears.

"No, Mr. Crow, no, how could they do this. That's horrible, horrible, horrible."

Mallard looked away as the tears streaked down his face and around his bill before dropping to the pond below. Crow put a hand around his neck and coughed to clear his throat. He put the pictures behind him on his desk.

"I'm sorry. I didn't mean to upset you so much. It's just that, well, this is what we're looking at Mr. Mallard if we can't get you off. Now, Parliament and Crown Council will say that they didn't actually do that to Mr. Atratus. At least not the last bit. His punishment was the clipping, but his death came at the hands of Mr. Vulpes Vulpes. Which is technically true, but if they hadn't have clipped him first, I believe he would still be alive today."

Mallard wiped his eyes and looked back at Mr. Crow.

"What did he do to deserve such a thing?"

Mr. Crow walked over to a side table and grabbed a tissue which he offered to Mallard when he returned. Mallard blew his nose and looked sadly at Mr. Crow through bloodshot eyes.

"He was charged with the same thing you have been charged with, though if I can be candid, his theatrics were far less outrageous than yours."

"And tell me again, please, what I've been charged with?"

"In simple law you have been charged with Unlawful Flight. Though more specifically you have been charged with Flying Without Proper Featherability."

"I don't understand what that means?"

Mallard looked at Mr. Crow through still wet eyes. He might be naïve but sadly, that was not a defense for breaking the law.

"It means, son, that you were flying not like the duck you are but like another bird. And that is, except for killing another member of Aves, the most heinous crime that one of us can commit."

Mr. Crow frowned and his jowls sagged. His days of practicing law were numbered and this trial would likely be one of the last. He was tired of trying to work within the system to instigate change. Hardly anything had changed since he had started almost fifty years ago.

"Do you think what I did was the most heinous crime next to murder?"

Mallard asked the question with sincerity. He wanted to be thought well of, especially by this old man who had become, over the last couple of days, like a grandfather to him. Mr. Crow shook his head slowly and sadly and shrugged as if he was only now unloading the burdens of the world.

"No, Mr. Mallard, I don't think what you did was heinous at all. This is an antiquated law that should be struck from the books, but I fear that day may still be far away. In the meantime, we need to move forward with a defense to try and get you off, and if we can't, then perhaps our best defense is to ask for forgiveness and leniency from the court."

Mallard looked down at his hands. He squeezed them together as if trying to wring out a wet towel.

"Did you defend that poor man, um...Mr. Atratus?"

"No, I didn't defend Mr. Atratus. I haven't lost a case yet, son, and I don't plan on you being the first. Now, we have to spend some time on coaching you through the trial and what to expect."

Mr. Crow looked at his watch, it was getting late in the day. The sun would soon be setting and Mr. Mallard and his friend would need to seek shelter for the night.

"When do you expect your friend to get here?"

Mallard shrugged.

"I don't know, I thought he'd be here by now. He said he would. Maybe he's had a change of heart."

As if on cue, the telephone rang and Mr. Crow answered it. His secretary, Ms. Pica Pica was on the other end.

"Yes, great news, please show him in Ms. Pica." Mr. Crow looked over at Mallard. "It appears your friend has arrived."

A few moments later, Ms. Pica opened the door to Mr. Crow's office and behind her entered Mallard's very small friend, Mr. Rifleman. Rifleman didn't look so good. His feathers were quite ruffled and he had some scrapes on his wings and a black eye.

"Rifleman!" said Mallard, rushing over to his friend as fast as his wobble would take him. "What have they done to you?"

Rifleman took Mallard's hand and he led him to a soft chair where he lay down. Rifleman's breath was belabored. He looked up at his friend and grinned.

"It's no big deal," said Rifleman.

"It certainly is. Tell me who did this to you?" asked Mallard.

"It was an abattoir of shrikes," said Rifleman, "led by the biggest asshole of them all, Lanius X. Cubitor."

"Good God," gasped Mallard, "where are they now?"

"I don't know," said Rifleman, regaining his composure, "a flock of robins came by and scared them off. Thank heavens."

"Yes, thank heavens," said Mr. Crow. "You're very lucky you know, they've been known to commit avesicide, though Parliament is clamping down on that."

Rifleman shook his head. Mr. Crow looked at Ms. Pica who was still by the open door.

"Can you get him some water, please," said Crow.

Ms. Pica nodded and left.

"No, I don't think they were intent on killing me. Lanius said I had to be careful what I said tomorrow or bad things would happen to me and my family."

"Who sent them?" asked Mr. Crow.

"I don't know, we weren't having a conversation, it was more like one of Lanius' soliloquies."

"Do you think we should take him to see Dr. Branta Canadensis?" asked Mallard.

"No, really, I'm okay," said Rifleman.

"You don't look too good," said Mallard.

"I think he's okay," said Mr. Crow. "These look like superficial scratches."

"See," said Rifleman, "I'm fine."

Ms. Pica came back in and offered a tall cool

glass of water to Mr. Rifleman. He drank it quickly and eagerly and gave it back to her when it was empty.

"Thank you," he said, his voice a song on the ear.

"That'll be all, thank you, Ms. Pica," said Mr. Crow.

Ms. Pica left the office and closed the door behind her.

"We don't have a lot of time. The sun will be setting within the hour and you chaps need to get home where it's safe before the Strigiformes come out and the other mammalian nocturnal carnivora."

Rifleman straightened himself up in the chair. Mallard pulled up another chair next to him and Mr. Crow stood in front of them pacing back and forth as if here were holding court. Which is really what this was all about. Getting these young men ready for tomorrow's theatrics.

"Maybe I should just try and plead it out," said Mallard. "I mean, look what they did to my friend

Rifleman."

Mr. Crow looked over at him sternly.

"Nonsense. This is exactly what they want. They want you to feel intimidated. First thing tomorrow I'll lodge a complaint with court security and inform them of this act of violence against my client's witness. I'm sure at the very least we can get some protection for you and Mr. Rifleman," said Crow.

Mallard looked over at his friend for reassurance. Rifleman looked back at him and smiled. He was a small fellow, Rifleman, much smaller than Mallard. What he lacked in size though, he more than made up for in courage.

"I'm here, aren't I? I'm not going to get intimidated by an abattoir of freaks."

Mallard nodded and smiled back at his old friend. Since they were in kindergarten they'd been inseparable.

"Are you sure?"

Rifleman nodded.

"Let's get on with it," he said.

Mr. Crow stopped pacing, his head down, staring at the floor deep in thought. He looked up at Mallard.

"Okay Mr. Mallard, tell me again from the beginning what happened. Don't leave anything out."

"Well," said Mallard, making himself comfortable in the soft chair next to his friend. "It started a month ago. On the the 18th of March actually."

"But we'd been messing around and having fun like that for much longer," interjected Rifleman looking pleased with himself.

"Yes, that's true," said Mallard, looking at Mr. Crow. "Do you want me to start earlier than that?"

Mr. Crow was pacing the floor back and forth, his hands clasped behind his back, his head bowed down, deep in thought. He stopped and looked up at Mallard.

"No, we don't need to invite more trouble. As far as the Parliament is concerned you did this just one time, on the day you were caught. March the

18th. Start with that day and just stick to that day. Please. If they know you've been up to these aerobatics and theatrics for longer than that, you'll just get into more trouble. Trouble we don't need."

"Okay, well, it was the eighteenth then. I'd met Rifleman at the south side of Blind Beggar's Pond."

Blind Beggar's Pond was not the pond that Mr. Crow's office looked out over. No, this was a much bigger pond. In fact, it was strange it had been named a pond, since it was over twenty five acres large and deep enough in its middle that you couldn't see the light from the very bottom. Not that Mallard knew that, he hadn't actually swum all the way to the bottom of the pond.

In fact, Mr. Mallard, and this was a secret he really was quite ashamed of, was scared of water. He did put on a brave face now and then, and he'd splash around in the ponds around Broken Beak Woods where he lived, just so the other ducks wouldn't think he was really weird.

But putting his head under water, that put the fear of the Velociraptor in him. But he had to do that sometimes too. Put his head under water and pretend. That's why Rifleman was his best friend. Rifleman didn't judge him for his peculiarities and Rifleman was a land bird, which meant they could spend as much time together as they liked in the sky and on the land and Mallard wouldn't have to worry about his fear of water.

And because Mallard didn't like water you could surmise that he didn't much like fish either. And you'd be right. Most of his family and his kin, ate a large quantity of fish. But not him. He couldn't stomach them. Even when his mother served him the best fish from the pond for dinner, he'd just poke and prod at it and eat the veggies and sides.

This gave his mother no end of grief. He might as well have been the Avian equivalent of a vegan. It worried his mother, but he grew up strong and healthy eating insects, small frogs and lizards, fruits, berries, grains and seeds, that in time Mallard's mother felt less concerned and learned how better to cook for him.

"I understand that you don't like water Mr. Mallard. Is this well known?" asked Crow.

"I don't think so, Mr. Crow, I mean Rifleman knows. But I don't think anyone else does. I've done my best to try and keep it hidden. That's one of the reasons we met at Blind Beggar's Pond. Just about every day I'd have to be at or near the pond, or a pond, just so other ducks didn't think I was a quack, if you'll pardon the pun."

Mallard chuckled at his own cleverness, Rifleman gave a good laugh, soft and round, like a jazz tune.

"A quack, is usually used when speaking of an incompetent physician," said Crow.

"Well, I think you get the idea, plus, I always like a good pun," said Mallard.

"Very well then, please carry on."

"I don't have many friends," said Mallard, looking down at his feet sheepishly. "Rifleman's my best friend...Actually he's my only friend. Most of the other ducks just tolerate me."

Mallard turned to look at Rifleman, a glint in

his eye and a smirk at the corners of his mouth.

"In fact," he continued, "you might say I'm a bit of an odd duck."

He could barely finish the sentence without breaking into a laugh and slapping his knee. He almost had Rifleman rolling on the floor laughing in fits. Even Mr. Crow had to smile. Mallard was after all, quite charming even if he was naïve.

"Very clever, Mr. Mallard, we get the picture. But we're not here at Crow and Black Bird Solicitors and Barristers for comedy hour. The day is quickly disappearing and you're due in court tomorrow morning. Let's not forget the severity of what lies ahead."

Mr. Crow's tone brought the laughter to an end. Mallard looked back up at Crow with a more sombre face this time before continuing.

"We met at the pond, Rifleman and I at just before sunup. It was such a beautiful morning Mr. Crow, wasn't it Rifleman?"

"Sure was," said Rifleman.

"The autumn air was crisp and cool, and while

I was waiting for Rifleman, looking over the dark pond I shivered. Most of the diurnal birds were only just getting up, yawning and stretching their wings. The nocturnal ones were settling in for a snooze. Only the crepuscular birds were out and about, but they're a minority and most of them are pretty solitary and quiet. It was a beautiful time. The sky was still, hardly a sound and the pond was like a sheet of glass. I almost thought I could walk on it. But I didn't, because I knew better."

"But you can practically walk on it," said Crow, "at least float on it on your belly."

"You haven't been listening, Mr. Crow. I'm awfully fearful of the water. I know it's strange but it's the truth. And the thought now, of floating along on top of the water, my feet paddling away like breadsticks below the surface for fish to eat, just sends shivers up my spine."

And it was true, Mallard actually shivered just sitting there thinking about it.

"Anyway, you were standing at the edge of Blind Beggar's Pond then, please carry on," said

Mr. Crow.

Mallard nodded.

"I didn't have to wait long. Rifleman is pretty punctual. We were meeting to watch the sun rise from thirty thousand feet."

Mr. Crow raised his eyebrow and his monocle almost fell out.

"You do know that your altitude limit Mr. Mallard as a duck is below twenty thousand feet?" asked Mr. Crow.

Mallard nodded.

"I do, but I wanted to take Rifleman up to see the majesty of a sunrise at thirty thousand feet. Very few birds have seen that, and the ones that can, just don't seem to appreciate the beauty."

"You mean the swans and geese that are licensed to fly above twenty thousand feet?"

"Well, what about Mr. Rüppel and his ilk that I've seen up there, even higher than thirty thousand feet. Nobody thinks anything of that, and Mr. Falco and friends who chased us up to over thirty thousand feet trying to kill us? What about them?"

Mr. Crow readjusted his monocle and squinted at Mallard through it.

"Mr. Rüppel has a special allowance for flight above twenty thousand feet as needed. Mr. Falco, when on duty, as I'm sure you are no doubt aware has total discretion as to speed and altitude, especially when chasing lawbreakers. And as much as I am sympathetic Mr. Mallard, you were breaking the law. An obtuse and outdated law to be sure, but it is the law we have to now use to get you free."

"I know, I'm just saying. We weren't hurting anybody, just out trying to have some fun and explore the limits of our capabilities. What's so wrong with that?"

Mr. Crow looked down thoughtfully before he answered Mallard.

"Son, there is nothing philosophically wrong with that. But you have to understand the fear that is entrenched in Broken Beak Woods. Folk around here are scared of change. They're scared of finding out they might be capable of more than they actually are. That carries great responsibility and most of our community are just happy being birds of a feather. Everyone in Broken Beak Woods has their place and that's how society has long prospered. At least that is the argument they'll use. A duck is not an eagle and shall not act like one."

"But, we're limiting our potential!" exclaimed Mallard. "Imagine how much better we'd all be, if we could just be who we are. If we were allowed to pursue our passions, even if that meant a duck soaring with the geese and swans or zipping along with the falcons. We'd have greater understanding Mr. Crow, don't you see? There'd be greatness here in Broken Beak Woods instead of mediocrity and soullessness."

Mr. Crow looked at Mallard and smiled at him. It was a warm but heartbroken smile.

"I agree with everything you say, Mr. Mallard. That's why I've taken your case pro bono. I want to help, but we have to work within the confines of what society allows us."

"No! That's giving up. Society will never move forward if individuals don't stretch themselves beyond their comfort levels first."

Mr. Crow shook his head slowly, smiling still.

"Do you know how our home got the name Broken Beak Woods?"

"No."

"Well then, let me tell you how our home got its name, so that we might better understand what we're up against."

Mr. Crow pulled up a third chair and looked over the big bough just behind where Rifleman and Mallard sat. Across the horizon the sun was slowly setting in the west. It was painting yellows, oranges and reds all across the low sky. A flock of gulls flew across the sun's ruddy face, threading it with white cotton. Mr. Crow cleared his throat.

"A long time ago, before your grandaddy, and even much longer before his grandaddy, my kin lived here amongst the others. Our home here at that time was called Aves Wet Woods. You probably get why it was called that. It had the

31

same number of ponds, from the great Blind Beggar's Pond to this little one we're looking over, called Squire's Spoon."

Below them, the little pond, Squire's Spoon was emptying and birds were taking flight to their nests.

"It is said that there was once a young crow named Blackened Blade. He wouldn't have been much older than you are now. Sometimes, in closed meetings and hushed voices, some of the older crows will talk about Blackened Blade's mythos. He was by all accounts a respectful, but hot headed, youngster who didn't respect most of the rules if they didn't make sense. And like today, many of those rules didn't make sense. I'll give you an example. Birds of a feather had to flock together, and that wasn't just about sticking and flying with your own kind, it was about who you could marry and have children with too."

"That's still how it is," said Rifleman. "That's why Mallard is doing what he's doing, to change things."

"Well, that's not really the only reason. I do what I do because that's how Zhengi made me. I just feel this is my destiny, the reason for being, how I am to manifest my soul."

"Ahem," said Mr. Crow.

Mallard and Rifleman looked up at the old man quietly.

"That law," continued Mr. Crow, "has changed, Rifleman. That is the reason you and Mallard can be friends. Though what the two of you got up to recently might put that in jeopardy. Back in the olden times, when Blackened Blade was around, the two of you could never have been friends, let alone fly around together. Now all that remains of that still archaic law is the marriage and mating aspect of it. And this goes to the very foundation of what these laws are really all about. They're about keeping control on society and managing, as best as they think they can, the destiny of society, even if that encroaches on the individuals."

Mallard put up his hand to ask a question.

"This is not school, Mr. Mallard, you don't need

to put up your hand to ask a question," said Mr. Crow.

"Well, I'm just trying to understand then, how not allowing me or anyone else to marry outside my kin harms society. I don't get it."

"These are the problems that many of us are trying to gently change, but this is what Parliament will likely tell you. We can't have ducks marrying geese and hawks marrying eagles because we don't know what will happen to their offspring. What if their offspring turn out to be imbeciles or worse, handicapped. That would be a terrible strain on society forced to look after them. That's their argument and that's why it is disallowed. We, Mr. Mallard, and I say we as society, understand ducks, we understand eagles, we understand sparrows, but we don't understand dugles or sprikes, offspring of sparrows and shrikes."

"That just seems ridiculous, sorry Mr. Crow, but I just don't get it. If Zhengi would allow sprikes to be born then he wouldn't allow them to be handicapped. Everything Zhengi made is beautiful and perfect, Mr. Crow."

Mr. Crow smiled at Mallard.

"Yes, if you believe in Zhengi. But I'd agree, whether you believe in Zhengi or nature, if sprikes came into this world, they'd likely be just as healthy as the rest of us. Have you heard of the Mongulls?"

Mallard nodded.

"I think so, but aren't they a myth?"

"No, Mr. Mallard, the Mongulls are not a myth. They were almost killed by Mr. Falco and friends way back, though after the time of Blackened Blade. It was after him that things took a dark turn for us. The Mongulls, if you know much about them, were a hardy, scrappy kin who married whoever they wanted. They bred outside their order. This was practically treasonous. In my youth, as an aside, I met a Mongull couple once. He was a Lapwing and she the most beautiful Albatross I ever met, even to this day. They shared a love that I have very rarely seen."

"Where are they now?" asked Rifleman.

Mr. Crow took out his monocle and let it dangle from his breast pocket.

"I don't know, young man, they are probably in hiding. There are very few Mongulls left and if the falcons or shrikes find them, there is an open and ongoing order to have them killed."

Mallard's face went pale and his mouth slacked open.

"What?"

Mr. Crow nodded solemnly.

"Yes, Mr. Mallard, I'm afraid it's true. There are ongoing problems that society needs to overcome. After the great Avialanic war that lasted three generations, the remaining Mongulls who had not been murdered, went into hiding. By some reliable scholarly estimates, over ninety percent of Mongulls were slaughtered in the Avialanic war. Though truth be told, it wasn't so much a war as it was a genocide."

"I can't believe it. So, they'll still murder our own kind if they find them?" asked Rifleman.

"Yes," said Mr. Crow, "though you won't find

the order in any official papers, it's just quietly understood amongst those who wield the power."

"But what if," said Mallard, "that by allowing intermarriage, it made us stronger? I mean there is just an equal chance that diversity will strengthen our species as much as it might handicap us."

"I agree, Mr. Mallard, and in fact I think, and some of the best scientific minds agree, that intermarriage would be most beneficial, not by developing a superior race but by increasing our DNA heritage and understanding. Plus, as these things happen, if they ever will, there is a greater chance of positive evolutionary change. In any event, we're getting a little off topic here, I just wanted to help put our fight in perspective. We have a long way to go, there are many asinine rules that are still on the books that need to be changed, and your case highlights one of them. Perhaps the trunk of these obtuse and unenlightened laws. If we can gain a small win with your case, it might, in time be seen as a larger victory for us all."

"Tell us more about Blackened Blade?" asked Rifleman, perking up and sitting taller in his chair. He loved to hear stories of heroic adventure.

Mr. Crow smiled and nodded.

"Very well then, let's get back to the story of Blackened Blade. Now, Parliament will deny this story as fact, and their official position is that it is a mythology created by the crows to make sense of their world. But perhaps more troubling is that Parliament thinks my kin made up this story to make ourselves out to be more heroic and daring than we are, but this is just plain false."

"I believe you, Mr. Crow," said Mallard.

"I know you do. So let me carry on with the telling of Blackened Blade. He was a young man, very similar in temperament to you. He was kind, never vengeful and he never hurt another soul, or not on purpose anyway. He respected the important rules like not stealing, killing or harming others, but some of these other rules he didn't seem to see the sense in. Now these were rules mind you, not yet laws. Parliament at this stage was more like a council of elders setting standards, but it hadn't evolved into the all powerful government we have now, with the power to tax us to death and mete out punishment for all sorts of punitive and trivial things."

Ms. Pica knocked at the door.

"Come in," said Mr. Crow.

"It's after five, Mr. Crow, and if you don't need me anymore, I'll be heading home if that's okay?"

"Yes, of course, thank you for your help, Ms. Pica."

She smiled at Mr. Crow and then turned to look at the two young men.

"You two stay out of trouble now until after the trial, okay?"

Mallard and Rifleman nodded.

"We will."

"Good night then, see you in the morning Mr. Crow."

And with that, the door closed behind her and the three of them sat together as the sun continued to slip towards the horizon.

"Now where was I?" said Mr. Crow, knowing full well where he was in this tale.

"You were telling us about Blackened Blade," said Rifleman.

Mr. Crow nodded and smiled.

"Oh yes, that's right. Blackened Blade was a dashingly handsome fellow, and the scar on his right cheek only made him look more mysterious and rakish."

"How did he get his scar?" asked Mallard.

"He got it from a near death dive he had taken trying to escape Mr. Falco and friends during one of his extreme flights. You have to understand that Mr. Falco and his friends weren't yet institutionalized as lawmen at that time, they were more like self-identified tough guys, with not much of a code of honor. Anyway, he had been flying like a daredevil, practicing all sorts of stunts. He was quite the showman, but humble with it and always encouraging others. He was doing some acrobatics when Mr. Falco and friends came upon him and ordered him to stop his daring. They started to dive bomb him and bang up against him during flight, even after he had promised to stop his acrobatics. But it seems like Mr. Falco and company were just hell-bent on making an example of him, so he had to flee, but they chased him hard. Mr. Falco as you know, since you've met him, is a terrific flyer and was thought to be the fastest diver in the world, until they came upon Blackened Blade."

"How fast could he go, Mr. Crow?" asked Rifleman full of excitement, his eyes practically popping out of his head.

"Some say, and this is how he got his name, that he was as fast as a blade falling from the sky, and since he was black, they named him Blackened Blade. There were many witnesses on the day Blackened Blade got his scar, both of my kin and others. Nowadays we know that Mr. Falco can dive at two hundred miles per hour. Well, when chased by them, Blackened Blade hurtled himself towards earth, far outstripping the falcons, but he narrowly pulled out of the dive just an oak's height off the ground after Mr. Falco had given up and he looked behind him just to check if they were still hot on his tail. They weren't, but when he looked back he almost collided with a big branch which would have killed him, except for his masterful flying skills. He narrowly missed it but a small branch off that same bough gouged his cheek and left him with that scar that he earned."

"Was he okay, did he need to see the doctor?" asked Rifleman.

Mr. Crow nodded.

"He did indeed and he needed thirteen stitches to sew back the wound."

"I bet I could dive faster than him," said Mallard. "I easily out flew Mr. Falco."

"Yes, Mr. Mallard, you did," said Mr. Crow. "But you still got caught despite your abilities and that's why you and I are here talking."

Mr. Crow paused and looked deeply into Mallard's eyes. He smile warmly and gently.

"And Zhengi knows you are the greatest flyer that ever lived. You know you broke the sound barrier?"

Mallard didn't say anything, but he grinned hearing that.

"They clocked you at Mach 1.11."

Mallard beamed.

"Incredible," he said. "Helped along by adrenaline. I was really scared of Mr. Falco catching me so I gave it all I had. I was wondering about that though, because I heard this boom like somebody had just banged a bass drum next to my head, and then all of a sudden, right after, it got really quiet. I couldn't hear anything, until I slowed back down again."

Rifleman put up his hand.

"Hit me here," he said.

They exchanged high fives.

"Okay, chaps," said Mr. Crow. "What you have accomplished is very inspiring but it is this inspiration as well as lack of respect for the law that is going to get you into a heap of trouble if we don't get all our ducks in a row for your defense."

Mr. Crow smiled, and Rifleman and Mallard

burst out laughing.

"Good pun, Mr. C," said Mallard.

Mr. Crow took a small bow as he sat in his seat.

"Tell us the rest of the story about Blackened Blade," said Rifleman.

"Well, as you can imagine, Mr. Falco and his cronies had it out for Blackened Blade ever after that. Nobody was going to usurp their position as the fastest divers in the world, so they kept a lookout for him whenever they could. But by now, all hell was breaking loose. Blackened Blade was somewhat of a celebrity and all sorts of birds were seeking him out for help on improving their skills and becoming the best flyers that they could. But they had to meet discreetly in private and during crepuscular hours when the falcons were less active and aware. This went on for months and Blackened Blade at the encouragement of others, mostly Mr. Swift, decided to set up an open competition. Mr. Swift you see, enjoys competition because he believes it makes everyone better, even if he was still the reigning fastest vertical flyer."

"Not anymore," said Rifleman, nudging Mallard.

"Yes, I am also aware you were clocked at a vertical speed in excess of one hundred and twenty miles an hour Mr. Mallard."

Mallard grinned like a proud school boy who had just got an A, his only A ever received.

"Didn't the falcons try to put a stop to the open competition?" asked Rifleman.

"They did, but by this time, the competition had caught the public's imagination and Mr. Falco couldn't get the support he needed to quash it."

"So what happened? Did Blackened Blade win, everything?" asked Rifleman, almost hopping up and down on his chair.

Mr. Crow shook his head.

"This is a story, Mr. Rifleman, of how our home got its name Broken Beak Woods. It is a story with an unhappy ending, I'm sorry to say."

Rifleman settled back down, deflated, as if he were a balloon that Mr. Crow had just popped.

"I don't think I want to hear the rest then," he said.

"I do," said Mallard.

"I understand," said Mr. Crow. "But it is a story that needs telling. So let me finish it up."

Rifleman looked away, folding his arms in front of his chest and slumping down deeper into his chair. Mallard put his arm around him and looked down at his small friend.

"It's okay," he said to Rifleman, "nothing's going to happen to me."

Rifleman slowly looked over and up at Mallard and smiled weakly as gravity grabbed at the corners trying to turn it into a frown. Mr. Crow looked at the two of them. An unlikely pair of friends you ever saw, yet such a loyal bond and caring between them. Though youthful enthusiasm and optimism was clouding them from seeing the very severity of Mallard's situation.

"You don't know that for certain," said Rifleman, "things could change. Mr. Crow said that you could have your wings clipped. What good is a bird with clipped wings, Mallard. I can't fight off every predator. I'd try though, but I'm just small..."

"Small, but brave, Rifleman," said Mallard, "you're the bravest person I've ever met."

Rifleman smiled more broadly that time, chuffed as a rooster at first dawn.

"Besides, many birds do okay without flying. I'll manage. If it comes to that, which I'm sure it won't, not when I have the esteemed Mr. Crow as counsel."

Mr. Crow smiled at Mallard bravely as the young man looked at him. What he was thinking inside was a much different thing. For the first time in his distinguished career he thought he might actually lose. That this could really be one for the books, and not a good one.

But Lord Tyto Alba was a harsh judge, and Parliament had of late become much stricter regarding matters of disorder and disobedience which Mallard's crime was surely, in their eyes, the most flagrant example that they'd see.

In fact, Mallard couldn't have chosen a worse

time in Avian history to conduct himself in such a risky manner. It was almost as if the perfect storm had conspired to punish not only Mallard but Crow himself for his unblemished success to this point. Not since Blackened Bird had one of their kind taken such bold steps at undermining the authority of Parliament. And back in Blackened Blade's day, these were rules and not laws, as such there was not the same kind of punishment that could be delivered as there was now.

"What is it, Mr. Crow?" asked Rifleman, looking at him with concern.

Mr. Crow had gotten all caught up in his thoughts and hadn't realized that both Rifleman and Mallard had stopped conversing a few moments ago, looking intently at him for him to continue the story of Blackened Blade and Broken Beak Woods. Mr. Crow looked up at them and smiled. Smiles, it seemed, were small feeble ghosts around Mr. Crow's office lately, dying in wisps and puffs.

"Oh, nothing, I was just noticing how late in

the day it's getting and we really need to get on with what we got together for."

"We're waiting for you to continue, Mr. Crow," said Mallard.

"Right. Well, where was I?"

Mr. Crow scratched at his graying temple and looked around the office.

"You were telling us about how the falcons weren't able to stop the open competition that Blackened Blade had set up."

"Oh yes. Well, it was a Sunday and the competition was scheduled for the whole day and well into the night. This was to allow for both nocturnal and diurnal competition. Blackened Blade wanted it to be fair. And you can't get the most out of a competitor if they haven't rested well enough, can you?"

"No," said Rifleman, his eyes wide as saucers, hanging on every last word of Mr. Crow's.

"At sunup the first races were begun. Blackened Blade, being one of the strongest competitors had decided that he would compete at night, in one of the last events."

"That doesn't seem smart," said Rifleman, "crows aren't usually nocturnal."

Mr. Crow sighed and nodded his head.

"I know, and in hindsight this was perhaps one of the biggest errors that Blackened Blade made, and it cost him his life."

"No!" exclaimed Rifleman. "I told you I wouldn't like this story. I don't want to hear any more."

Mallard put his hand on his friend's shoulder.

"I think we need to hear it, if only as a warning."

Rifleman looked off to his left. He folded his arms in front of him again. He was looking away from Mallard.

"I think it is important, Mr. Rifleman, if you want to truly help your friend, I think you should listen to the rest. You only got roughed up by Lanius because that was their plan. They could have easily killed you. We aren't only up against Parliament but we're also up against others who don't care for following the law when they think their way of life is being threatened."

"Okay," said Rifleman, looking back at Mr. Crow. "I'll listen to the rest."

"Good, because you're our key witness and your help is crucial if we are to win this case."

Rifleman nodded.

"The competition was divided into three categories. Birds could compete in only one of them. There was Horizontal Speed, Vertical Speed and then there was Freestyle. Freestyle being a combination of both Horizontal and Vertical with acrobatics and all sorts of other skills that the individual bird felt they wanted to use."

"I think I could do well in that category," said Mallard.

"Except," said Mr. Crow, "that competitions are strictly forbidden and you're in trouble for trying as it is. Really, Mr. Mallard, you need to appreciate the severity of the situation that you're in."

"I do, it's just unfair, that's all. I mean why I can't I be who I am and fly how I want. We'd all be better off if we could manifest our soul's destinies, Mr. Crow."

"I know, son," said Mr. Crow, "but for now and the next day you need to try, if you can, and I know it'll be hard, to show remorse. Without remorse, we might as well take you to Dr. Branta Canadensis and have him clip your wings before the trial even starts."

"Fine, I'll try," huffed Mallard.

Mr. Crow ignored the theatrics. The more he spent time with Mallard the more he realized how similar he was to Blackened Blade. In fact, if he believed in reincarnation he would swear he was dealing with the incarnation of Blackened Blade. At the very least, they were birds of a feather. And this concerned him deeply. Not because he thought that Mallard would end up dying like Blackened Blade, but because he thought that Mallard would be severely punished for his outrageous behavior and lack of remorse.

These were difficult times in Broken Beak Woods. Food was scarce due to some unknown pathogen in the environment and Parliament was taking a very heavy-handed approach to anyone breaking the rules.

"Now the Freestyle event was the big event that everyone was really watching and looking forward to. It was the last event to take place in the evening and the one for which the largest prize was to go to."

"What was that prize?" asked Rifleman.

"That prize, my young man, was fours per day of unimpeded flight for the following thirty days. The victor could choose which four hours in each day they wanted that to be, but they had to be consecutive hours."

"What do you mean when you say unimpeded flight?" asked Mallard.

"It meant that no birds, no one, except for the victor could be flying during those hours. Basically, the heavens and the deep blue sky was the sole domain of the victor for those four hours."

"Incredible," said Rifleman. "I can't believe it. I've never heard of anything so grand in all my life."

Mr. Crow smiled at the youngster and folded his hands in his lap.

"I know, those were heady and very different times. In any event, that never came to be because of what happened during the last event."

"So nobody won?" asked Rifleman.

"Not legally. The whole Freestyle event turned into a free for all and became quite nasty. But let me get to that in due time. I need to tell the story in the way that it happened."

"I'm all ears," said Mallard.

"The open competition brought out almost the whole community to watch. Sure you had a few stick in the muds who didn't want to participate or even support the competitors but just about everyone else, ninety percent of the community came out to watch."

"Who won the individual events?" asked Rifleman.

"I'm getting to it," said Mr. Crow, smiling at Rifleman's enthusiasm. "There weren't a lot of upsets or surprises, but what the legend says of that day is that there was a tremendous camaraderie amongst all who entered. All sorts of records were broken. For example, Mr. Rifleman, a great, great, great etc. grandmother of your kin broke the record for the longest flight for a Tītipounamu. She remained airborne and flew for over one hundred miles, covering that distance in less than three hours."

Rifleman sat up taller in his chair, his eyes bright with hope and pride.

"I'd say, that in fact, just about all of our different species broke records that day. We began to learn what we were really capable of, what we might be able to accomplish. The tone of the event was electric, it spurred our imaginations. We started to imagine all sorts of potentialities we might become capable of, until the last event. Which I'll get to in a moment."

Mallard was listening intently, he reveled in the heroics of Blackened Blade, it inspired him. In fact, he was more intent on inspiring change in society than he had ever before. What had started as a mere thoughtless exercise for him and Rifleman to have some fun, was now a calling. What had merely been a way of stretching his wings, had changed into a philosophy and a petition to inspire his kind to untold greatness they had up to this point been fearful of.

Mr. Crow on the other hand, hoped that the story of Blackened Blade would cool Mallard's jets, at least enough to get them through the trial with an outcome that didn't involve the punishment of clipping. That was as good as a death sentence. Maybe he could ask for banishment. Harsh, to be sure, but under the circumstances, he'd consider it a win.

"As I said earlier, there weren't many upsets. Both the winners of the Vertical Speed and Horizontal Speed were the favorites of the day."

"Who won them," squealed Rifleman.

"Well, as you can imagine, first place and golden feather, was awarded to Mr. Swift. He also set a new horizontal speed record, though legend has it that he wasn't flying as hard as he could. Mr. Swift entered the record books with a speed flight of one hundred and twenty four miles per hour. Mr. Swift was also the only bird to take two trophies, not just for speed but for distance traveled during the competition. During those twelve hours, Mr. Swift flew one thousand two hundred and thirty four miles."

Rifleman whistled.

"Wow, that's just incredible. I get tired just thinking about it."

Mr. Crow smiled.

"I know, it was really inspiring what we managed on that day. I often wonder what we'd be capable of today if we had managed to encourage each other to continue use our talents and skills to the fullest all these many years later. To reach beyond what we thought was possible."

"Well, that's what I'm trying to do," said Mallard. "I'm trying to show everyone what's possible. It isn't scary to push yourself, to try and become more than you think you're capable of.

Even if you reach for the stars, Mr. Crow, and fall short, you might still make it to the moon."

Mr. Crow smiled at Mallard, though his eyes were misty with sadness.

"I know, son, I know. I just don't think now's the time to push the boundaries so hard, not when society is fearful and you have rigid and conservative judges in Parliament."

Mallard looked at Mr. Crow and his eyes burned with anger. Not at the old lawyer but at a society that thought it best and even wise to hold them back from their full potential. Just because it was risky and the outcome unknown.

"It's never a good time, Mr. Crow. And it wasn't even like I was trying to be anti-authoritarian, I was just trying to do what came natural to me. Trying to stretch my wings and reach my potential. With all the hue and cry about it you'd think I'd killed someone."

Mr. Crow placed his monocle back on and turned around towards his desk to find some papers. He shuffled through them, slowly, taking a look at each one until he found what he was looking for.

"Son," he said looking at Mallard. "These judges in Parliament are not playing games. They are using the most severe punishments for the smallest of crimes."

Mr. Crow started scanning the paper in front of him.

"Do you know how many alleged crimes there are for which clipping is deemed an appropriate punishment?"

He looked up at both Rifleman and Mallard and his one black eye, glimmered large like a black hole behind the monocle. Mallard thought he might lose himself and be swallowed up in its depths. He shook his head.

"No," said Rifleman.

"Twenty seven," answered Mr. Crow. "And the worst of it, is that most of these involve nothing but petty infractions."

He looked back down at the paper in his hands.

"Here's a good example. You can get your wings clipped for flying too loudly. And how on Earth do they determine that? What about this one, flying directly over Mr. Falco's business and residence. Or, this one, which is my favorite, flying outside of official flight hours."

"What does that even mean?" asked Mallard.

"Basically, that if you're a nocturnal bird and you're caught flying during the day, you'll have your wings clipped."

Mallard shook his head.

"And you want us to play it safe, while the whole of our society here at Broken Beak Woods is coming more and more under the authoritarian and fascist control of Parliament. A parliament which is supposed to allegedly have been elected to represent us and yet, we haven't had an election in over nine years."

"They're calling for an election next year," said Mr. Crow.

"Right," said Mallard, "like they've been doing for five years now."

Crow had to admit that Mallard had a point. Parliament, it seemed, had suspended elections for five years now. Most of the community grumbled, but with such a long history of living within strict boundaries, laws and regulations, most of the birds out there didn't want to ruffle any feathers. Especially since times had been good. Well, they were good that is, until about a year ago when the Hollow Hunger started. Which, coincidentally coincided with Parliament's cracking down of the law.

"Do you want to know how many birds, just in this last year, Parliament has punished with clipping?"

"Not really," said Mallard.

"Well, I'm going to tell you anyway."

Mr. Crow looked down and his beak moved quietly as he started to count.

"Eleven thousand two hundred and one."

He looked up at Mallard and Rifleman. Rifleman's eyes were wide and scared, the whites showing, and he swallowed uncomfortably.

Mallard looked down and shrugged.

"And none of them. None of those more than eleven thousand, committed anything near to what you have committed with Flying Without Proper Featherability. If we have any chance of getting you off, we need to show some deference to the court. Now I know that's going to be hard for you. You'll have to swallow some of your pride. But I'm telling you, son, these judges are out to make an example of you. And if you get clipped, well, I fear they might as well just have given you a death sentence. Ninety nine percent of those eleven thousand I just told you about who got clipped for much lesser crimes than you, are dead within three weeks. And the rest will likely not see the rest of their natural lives. This is serious."

"What's serious, Mr. Crow, with all due respect," said Mallard, "is that Parliament is daily strangling our necks and trying to keep us from advancing. In fact, the more I think about it, they just want to keep us down. Self evolved individuals are more of a threat, if only because they are pushing us to greater heights, and that scares the old guards."

"I'm not going to argue with you," said Crow. "But I believe it would be better if you take a deferential position so that you might actually live out the rest of your days where you can do good work with the underground."

Rifleman nudged Mallard with his elbow.

"I think you should listen to him, Mal"

Mallard looked over at his friend.

"I am listening to him, Rife, but that doesn't mean I agree."

"Please, Mal, I'm begging you to heed his advice. I don't want to lose you and if you get clipped, how are you going to be able to escape predators, and perhaps more worrying, the Abattoir of Shrikes and rogue element of the Cast of Falcons?"

Mallard looked down at his hands and he clasped them together. He wrung them dry of blood until they were white and smooth as bone. He gritted his teeth and sighed like a slow moving, hot leveche.

"Fine," he said, not looking at anyone.

"It's for your own good. For the good of all of us," said Mr. Crow, looking kindly at Mallard, his big black eye wobbling like a dying treadle behind his monocle. "Sometimes, son, we have to lose the fight to win the war."

Mallard didn't say anything. He looked over his shoulder and the sun was shimmering not far above the horizon. He wanted to fly right to it, to hell with everything, he might as well burn up his wings like Icarus, if he was giving up.

"Tell us about the rest of the competition," said Rifleman, unaware of the seething anger slowly uncoiling like a Leviathan beneath Mallard's still facade.

"Yes, we should finish up the story of the open competition. As I said before, not many upsets occurred, but most of our species broke species-specific records. Mr. Swift was the only one to win two awards that day. But perhaps the most thrilling event, next to the Freestyle event was the

Vertical Speed event. Do you know who's the fastest bird in Broken Beak Woods?"

"I am," said Mallard.

"I meant, officially. Who's the fastest bird officially?"

"I know," said Rifleman, "I know."

Rifleman was practically bouncing up and down in his chair, eager to answer the question, his excitement bubbling over him like champagne.

"Tell, Mr. Rifleman."

"Mr. Falco and his kin."

Crow smiled at the young man and nodded his head.

"Very good, Mr. Rifleman, very good indeed. And that is the right answer. But up until that point on that day's competition there had not been as close a race as the Vertical Speed event. In fact, both Mr. Falco Peregrinus and Mr. Aquila Chrysaetos broke the previous vertical speed record which had been two hundred and thirty nine miles an hour."

"Wow, that's amazing," said Rifleman, leaning

in, his attention fully held by Crow's telling of the tale.

"I know."

"What speeds did they achieve?" asked Rifleman.

"Well, this event wasn't an upset, so Mr. Falco won, but only by a hair. It was practically a photo finish. Mr. Aquila came in at two hundred and forty seven miles an hour and Mr. Falco reached the giddy speed of two hundred and forty nine. From what the legend says of this event it was like nothing ever seen before or since. Some of the female species in attendance fainted watching those two cross the finish line almost neck and neck."

Rifleman rubbed his face. He could imagine the scene, the crowds electric and on the edges of their seats. The roar of the crowd like yelling lions. The dive bombing birds swooping down towards the crowds like stones thrown by Zhengi. Rifleman wondered how fast he had reached on Mallard's back before he bailed. He'd like to think he almost got that fast.

"That's nothing, they clocked me at more than three times that," said Mallard.

"How fast do you think we were going before you told me to jump off?" asked Rifleman.

Mallard looked at his friend and grinned.

"I bet at that point we were almost going as fast as Mr. Falco."

"Wow, that was so thrilling. Too bad it's illegal."

Rifleman looked back to Mr. Crow.

"Tell us the rest of the story, Mr. Crow, I want to hear about Blackened Blade."

"Yes, we're just about there. The last event of that day was the Freestyle event, the event that Blackened Blade had saved himself for. He wanted to win this event hands down, so he had not taken part in the Vertical Speed or the Horizontal Speed events. Some historians who have studied the legend think that Blackened Blade could have won the Vertical Speed event. At least based on what speeds he was reaching just before the catastrophe that cost him his life."

Crow turned back around to his desk and placed the papers he had been holding back down. He lit an old gnarled candle, almost a replica of the great oak's trunk that his office was perched on. He turned back to Rifleman and Mallard and took off his monocle.

"It was eight at night when the Freestyle competition started. There were several elimination rounds before the final round which got started at ten that evening. The Freestyle event had been scheduled so that Mr. Falco and Blackened Blade would only meet in the final round. It was well known that the two of them had it out for each other, mostly on Mr. Falco's part, but Blackened Blade knew how to throw down an insult too."

"Who was in the final round?" asked Rifleman.

"There were only six places in the final round for those who had made it. Blackened Blade of course, then Mr. Falco, Mr. Aquila, Mr. Gyr-Falco, Mr. Needletail and Mr. Swift. Blackened Blade had handedly won all his events as had Mr. Falco and Mr. Aquila. The elimination rounds for the rest of the contenders had been much closer. In fact, the race was really being watched only to see the outcome of the top three..."

"Blackened Blade, Mr. Falco and Mr. Aquila?" asked Rifleman.

"Yes, that's right. But the real competition was going to be between Mr. Falco and Blackened Blade. However, Mr. Falco was a sore loser and more than that, he was a mean spirited bird. Unknown to Blackened Blade, Mr. Falco had stationed some of his kin high in the upper branches of the three-hundred-foot Sierra Redwoods which were close to the finish line."

"What were they doing there?" asked Rifleman.

"You'll see. In the meantime, in the interest of safety and fairness many crows and falcons were circling high above the competition's sky. Some put them at around ten thousand feet up. There was some bumping and jostling, but all in all, the crows and falcons up there were supposed to be acting as marshals to keep the competition fair. Many of the owls, who up to this point had been the only protesting voices to the competition had come out to watch. They were perched high up in the trees, within hearing distance of the falcons. The Legend of Blackened Blade says that the owls, though not in on the sabotage that was to come, were nonetheless privy to it and should have intervened to stop it. Though as you'll come to see, it benefited their cause."

Mallard had slumped back into his chair, arms folded in front of his chest. Listening politely, but no longer really interested in the Legend of Blackened Blade. Rifleman however, was craning his little neck up towards Crow, catching each word as if they were rare, polished gems.

"At ten o'clock that night, the fireflies signaled the start of the race. They all headed out neck and neck as fast as a smudge, doing all sorts of theatrical and acrobatic swirls, turns and somersaults. It really was something to see. It didn't take long for the leading three to break off from the pack, with Blackened Blade already taking an early lead."

"What did the course look like?" asked Rifleman.

"It was thirty-three miles long with obstacles placed so as to require great acrobatic ability. The event required three turns through the course and had a vertical climb and drop of over one and a half miles. On their descent they'd skim the tops of those giant Redwoods and climb as high as the marshals at just over ten thousand feet."

"Who was winning? Was it Blackened Blade?" asked Rifleman.

Crow nodded his head and smiled.

"Yes, Blackened Blade had the lead by about a body length during the first round with Mr. Falco hot on his heels. By this time, Mr. Aquila had dropped a distant third, he was about seven body lengths behind Mr. Falco, the obstacle buoys were conducive to his larger size."

Rifleman looked over at Mallard. Mallard

looked back down at him.

"How's that hey? Blackened Blade winning the race, like a young Mr. Crow."

Mallard smiled and nodded.

"I'm not sure Mr. Crow was much of the athletic type."

"I was once. A long time ago when I was much younger than either of you, but an accident broke my wing and I've never had the same enthusiasm or ability since then."

"Sorry," said Rifleman, his face turning into sympathetic softness.

"It's okay," said Mr. Crow. "It was a long time ago and I learned my lesson."

"I'd like to hear the rest of the Legend of Blackened Blade," said Mallard.

"Yes. So during the first round Blackened Blade had a slight lead, the first descent he had reached two hundred and forty miles an hour. Now you have to understand that this was an obstacle course of sorts too, so you weren't likely to see the same speeds as in the pure Vertical

Speed event. Nevertheless, these were astonishingly fast times. But coming into the second round, Blackened Blade was jockeyed by Mr. Falco into an obstacle buoy and he took a bit of a rough tumble."

"No!" exclaimed Rifleman.

"Sadly yes, but he came out of it and still managed to hold onto second place, barely a body length ahead of Mr. Aquila and by this point about six body lengths behind Mr. Falco. As you can imagine, he was quite upset at being jockeyed by Mr. Falco around that corner, but the marshals, who were bickering with each other, hadn't noticed."

Mr. Crow got up and paced across the room in front of Rifleman and Mallard, his hands clasped behind his back.

"Coming into the third and final round, he had caught up with Mr. Falco and heading into the first corner he offered Mr. Falco the same courtesy he had been given before. However, Mr. Falco was ready for just such a thing and tucked down and behind, rather than being bumped into the buoy. It was enough to edge him into first place, leading again by about a body length. Blackened Blade looked back, Mr. Falco had hate in his eyes, but Blackened Blade knew he had the win, if he could just keep his speed up and keep Mr. Falco at bay."

"And could he?" asked Rifleman.

"Yes, things went very well, he soared, swiveled and somersaulted through that last round like a dancer, it was magnificent to watch a crow of all birds with such grace and finesse," said Mr. Crow.

He stopped then, deep in thought at the grandeur his people had known once. When the Congress of Crows was still a force to be reckoned with. A force of good and justice, the counterpoint to the Parliament that now had grown so fat, corrupted and bloated on power.

"Carry on, Mr. Crow, please carry on," said Rifleman.

Crow looked up at him and smiled, though his eyes looked at Rifleman through mists of sadness.

The last part was always the hardest in the retelling. He cleared his throat and reached for the glass of water that was on his desk. He took a sip and continued.

"He was on the last descent when he heard Mr. Falco's squawk. It sounded like a last ditch attempt to scare off Blackened Blade, but Blackened Blade wasn't easily scared. But that was not its intent anyway. It was the rallying cry to his mates in the Redwoods. A cast of falcons flew up towards Blackened Blade, hard to see in the dark night. They came at him like darts and jostled and pecked at him until he lost control. The marshals noticed this and headed down to help. The crow marshals were chased by the falcon marshals and a whole angry mess erupted in the sky that Blue Moon Sunday night."

"What happened to Blackened Blade?" asked Rifleman, his voice soft, scared of the answer.

"Blackened Blade was jostled so hard, they broke one of his wings and he lost control of his dive. Sadly, he smashed against large rocks on the cliff edge and legend has it he fell to his death into the valley below."

"No! No, no," said Rifleman, covering his eyes, hoping that he could stop it from happening.

"Yes, son, I'm sorry to say that's what happened to Blackened Blade. But more than that, on that Blue Moon Sunday, thirteen crows were thrashed against the Redwoods, their beaks broken and bloody, their days numbered as they slowly died of starvation."

Rifleman started to cry, softly, mumbling to himself.

"No, that's not right, that can't happen," he said.

He had his face in his hands, and Mallard rubbed his back tenderly.

"That's how we got the name for our home, Broken Beak Woods, thanks to the sacrifices of those fourteen crows. A sacrifice that was mostly in vain. For after that, Parliament usurped power from the Congress, though for some years after they kept up appearances by allowing a Congress filled with Parliament lackeys. It was shameful and disgraceful. Until society was so numbed and dulled into thinking that Parliament had their best interests at heart that they hardly noticed when Congress was abolished."

Crow looked off into the distance, far away, towards the horizon. But he wasn't looking at anything in particular, his mind was blank, a void of sadness at what had once been a vibrant community.

"What happened to Congress?" asked Mallard, squeezing Rifleman's shoulder as he tried to get ahold of himself.

Mr. Crow looked at Mallard and blinked his black eyes.

"Sorry, son, what did you ask?"

"I wanted to know what happened to Congress."

"Congress was abolished by the Parliament. Tyto Alba and his cronies quietly closed us down, like I said."

"I meant to say, what happened to the

members of Congress."

"Oh, yes. Well, most of us, who had been lawyers, like me, went back to practicing the law. Taking cases like yours that we thought could help move society forward. Sadly, in hindsight, that seemed like a naïve and overly optimistic hope."

"And the others?"

"The others..."

Mr. Crow paused and looked around. He walked over to the door and opened it. The reception area was quiet, Ms. Pica had left. He came back over to Rifleman and Mallard, walked behind them and closed the large window that was at their backs. He walked to Mallard's right side and closed a smaller window there. Then he went to his desk and put on the radio. Soft, mellow jazz was playing, the announcer introduced the group as the Whistling Thrush Quartet. A new and upcoming jazz band enjoying rave reviews.

All the while Mallard was looking at Mr. Crow as he walked around the office locking down everything as securely as he could. This Mr. Crow, old and wizened as he might be, certainly seemed a little odd and eccentric to Mallard. By the time Crow sat back down in front of Rifleman, both he and Mallard had deep furrowed brows.

"You never know who might be listening," said Mr. Crow.

"If you say so," said Mallard.

"Mr. Mallard, you have no idea how serious Parliament is taking these infractions. I showed you a picture of Cygnus Atratus and you still think we have an easy case ahead of us. I told you about the more than eleven thousand who have, just in this year, been clipped and you still can't accept the severity you find yourself in."

"I understand, but you're the best. You said so yourself, you've never lost a case."

"And this might be the first if I don't get you to help yourself."

"But with everything you're telling me, what's the point? Parliament seems to be strangling our freedoms more every day. They're taking a harder stance on those who break the law and they're looking to make examples. Who better than me for breaking one of their most serious laws? We might as well go out fighting, maybe we can inspire a revolution?"

Crow shook his head and sighed.

"I don't think society is ready yet for a revolution. Not enough people are hurting. Parliament is doing just enough lip service to keep most of the grumbling to a dull murmur. But the time is coming, though it might still be a year away, when enough of us are hungry, nay, starving in both the literal and metaphorical sense that a revolution can be ignited, but that isn't going to happen by the end of the trial."

"So you're saying it's hopeless then, basically?" asked Mallard.

"No, that's not what I'm saying. Just hear me out. You asked earlier what happened to the others in Congress, the ones who weren't lawyers. Well, the reason I went around closing everything and turning on the radio is because you don't know who's listening. The truth, and this is our greatest weapon because it is our greatest secret, is that the others have gone underground..."

"Well, what good is that?"

"Dammit, Mr. Mallard, your hotheadedness is going to get you into trouble just like it did Blackened Blade. The underground is working at the grassroots, recruiting and educating. It's a slow process but it's working. Membership is already in the hundreds of thousands. The Congregation, as it is called, is working steadily and tirelessly, but their work can only continue and advance if it remains secret."

Rifleman had regained his composure and was staring up at Mr. Crow.

"I'd like to join," he said.

"We'd love to have you," said Mr. Crow.

"And what does all of this have to do with me and my trial?" asked Mallard.

"Everything," said Crow. "First of all, there might be a chance of getting you off. You see, even the state controlled paper, the Tytonidae Times had grumbled recently about the heavy handed approach that Parliament has been taking. And I think they're looking for an opportunity to show compassion. This case of yours could be a grand example for them to show leniency and curry favor amongst the dissenting voices even within their own ranks."

"So you want me begging for Parliament's favor?"

"If you want to put it that way, then yes, I want you to try and show real remorse and regret and to throw yourself at the court's mercy. If you can do that, the worst case I imagine is that you'll get community service or perhaps six months jail time, but you'll still have your wings. Then what we do, is have you join the Congregation and go underground to help create the groundswell of support that, if all goes well, can start the revolution and bring down Parliament, which you're so eager to see."

"And what if they still take a hard stance against me, all your plans go out the window and I still get clipped."

"Son, that is the risk we have to take. It might happen, but if you show remorse and humility, you minimize the risk of that outcome. If you choose not to, then I can almost guarantee you'll be clipped. And that as we all know, might as well be a death sentence."

Mallard sighed and looked over at Rifleman.

"You should do what Mr. Crow says you should," said Rifleman. "Then we can both still be together working in the Congregation."

Mallard smiled and looked down at his small, brave friend. Then he looked back up at Mr. Crow and nodded.

"You make a lot of sense, Mr. Crow, I'll do what you suggest."

"Good, it will be for your best, for the best of all of us. Congregation is doing great work, we're really gaining momentum and we'll have the revolution you seek. It's just not going to happen in the next several weeks. We need, and we want it to be effective and it can only be effective if we strike at the right time, when Parliament is least suspecting it and when we have the support of the majority of citizens."

"Okay, I'll do it."

"Good, now before I let you go, we need to go over the events that transpired on the 18th of March. You said you had been waiting by Blind Beggar's Pond at just before sunup for Rifleman?"

Mr. Crow reached behind him and grabbed a legal pad and a pencil.

"Yes that's right. Rifleman was punctual like he usually is, except for today..."

"Hey," said Rifleman, "I was roughed up by Lanius, that's why I was late."

Rifleman thumped Mallard on the shoulder. Mallard chuckled.

"I was only teasing," he said, looking down at his friend. "Anyway, Rifleman got there just in time. We spent a moment just enjoying the quietness of the pond and the crispness in the air. The pond looked like thick ink in that dark sky, Occasionally, you'd see a small fish flopping up out of the water, breaking its surface before falling back down. It was truly enthralling."

Mr. Crow nodded and smiled. Dusk and dawn or twilight were often his very favorite times of the day. Like right now, the sun perched carefully on top of the horizon, balancing its orange rotundness upon the edge of the world like a ball rolling off a table.

"We must have just stood there at the edge of the pond for about five minutes."

Mallard looked down at Rifleman.

"Yeah, about five minutes, certainly no more," said Rifleman.

"We didn't even need to say a thing to each other," continued Mallard, "I just gave him a look and we took off towards the east, flying higher and higher in large arcs as we gained height. It's amazing the temperature differences as you get higher, like flying through blankets of warm air and then crisp cool temperatures. It's part of the thrill."

"It also gets very cold up there," said Rifleman.

"Yeah, really cold, but you can find some vents

that will take up to fifty degrees Fahrenheit off the temperature. I remember once, I went up to thirty three thousand feet and it must have been close to minus fifty Fahrenheit. As you can imagine, I didn't stay up there long at those temperatures."

"Do you think it was that cold when we went up?" asked Rifleman.

Mallard shook his head and laughed.

"No way, Rife, I wouldn't do that to you, I don't think you'd be able to stand that kind of cold. I reckon it was maybe at most minus ten. I did my best to follow a warm air chimney all the way up there."

"Really, still felt much colder to me," said Rifleman.

"I know, minus ten is still pretty cold. But believe me, you wouldn't have lasted long at minus fifty. And the thing is, Mr. Crow, we flew up there and almost immediately started our descent."

"Well, actually," said Rifleman, "I only flew up to about one mile and then you gave me piggyback the rest of the way."

"True. He was finding it hard, and I understand that. The effort is tremendous for a small bird to get much higher than that. So I carried Rife the rest of the way up. I think we almost got to ten miles. Definitely we made it past thirty thousand feet."

Rifleman was nodding his head.

"It was so incredible, Mr. Crow, you have no idea. The beauty and the majesty of the view up there."

"I can imagine," said Mr. Crow.

"The best part of flying so high up is that you can enjoy dawn for like a half hour or even more. Because what happens is that when you're so high up, you're the first to see the sunrise before anyone else. Right?"

Mallard looked down at Rifleman grinning. Rifleman grinned back and nodded.

"Tell him about how we made the sun bounce like a ball."

"Yeah, that's a neat trick. So you get up to ten miles or so and you can see the sun start to peek its sleepy eye above the horizon, and then what you do, is you dive bomb a few hundred feet, maybe even a thousand feet and the sun goes back to sleep. It's like you're Zhengi, creating the world, switching on and off the sun. You're playing hide and seek with the sun. And then you fly back up ten miles and the sun starts rising faster than it normally would. Then you dive bomb back down another thousand feet or so, you've gotta do this real quick, like under thirty seconds, and the sun, instead of rising, starts retreating. Like he's waking up, but then thinks, nah, I'm tired I'll just hit the snooze."

Rifleman was giggling and nodding his head up and down, trying to demonstrate how the sun was a bouncing ball.

"So we did that for a few minutes. Now you see the sun, now you don't. Right?"

"Yeah, I loved that. I wish we could do it again," said Rifleman.

"We will. And then after we'd done that for a while, we just watched the sun rise, almost in slow motion, almost like it wasn't. Because when you're up that high, you can start slowly descending and adjusting the speed at which the sun rises. Because as you descend you're descending the sun with you, so you can put it on pause and enjoy the sunset for a really, really long time."

"Except that didn't happen with us, did it?" said Rifleman.

Mallard shook his head and gritted his teeth. Flames flickered behind his eyes.

"No, it didn't work out how we wanted it to. At around twenty seven thousand feet we bumped into Mr. Rüppel by accident and I'm pretty sure he's the one who ratted us out. Though at around twenty five thousand feet we bumped into Dr. Branta Canadensis and friends, but he didn't seem angry to see us up there, and it was very shortly after that when Mr. Falco and cronies appeared."

"Did Mr. Rüppel say anything to you?" asked Mr. Crow.

"No, but he looked really upset, didn't he Rife?"

Rifleman nodded and pinched his lips together.

"He sure did, and he took off right away after seeing us. So I'm pretty sure it was him who ratted us out."

Mr. Crow nodded.

"What time would you say this was at?"

Mallard half shrugged and squeezed his mouth off to one side.

"I don't know for sure, but I'd probably say it was just before seven thirty. I'm pretty sure it was around seven thirty when the cops showed up."

Mr. Crow nodded solemnly and scribbled the information down on his yellow legal pad.

"Carry on."

"Well, we were down at around twenty three thousand feet by the time that Mr. Falco showed up..."

"That's interesting," said Mr. Crow, reaching behind himself and grabbing some papers on his desk, "because on these charges here, it says you were charged with flying above thirty thousand feet. Which you were, but you're saying that nobody actually saw you that high up, right?"

"Yes, Mr. Rüppel was only up around twenty seven thousand."

"Okay, good, that can help us. Carry on."

"So, I saw Mr. Falco coming off from the east. It was hard to see him because he was right in the sun coming towards me. He was practically on top of us when I saw him, and that's when I took a dive straight down and he came right after us."

"Did he identify himself as law enforcement?" asked Mr. Crow.

Mallard nodded and grinned sheepishly.

"He did, but he looked really pissed, I didn't want to stop for him for fear of my safety."

"Why not?"

"Because he had three other cops with him and they already had their pepper spray, batons and tasers out. I've heard the police are getting more brutal every day, beating suspects before asking questions and these four looked like that was exactly what they were going to do, so I bailed. And just think about what they could do to my friend Rife."

Mr. Crow nodded, writing steadily on his pad.

"They came after me with a vengeance, at one moment I thought they'd catch me. I got scared, because Rifleman was hanging onto me for his dear life and I knew I couldn't go as fast as I wanted, because he'd be torn off me at around three hundred miles an hour. So when we got down to around fifteen thousand feet, I asked him to bail."

"Did you?" asked Mr. Crow.

Rifleman nodded.

"I did, it was the scariest thing I ever did. I tumbled and tumbled for at least a mile before I could stabilize myself at around fifteen hundred feet. By that time, I couldn't find Mallard anywhere, and the cops were long gone. When I bailed, I couldn't see what was going on, I was just struggling to find balance."

"I understand," said Mr. Crow.

"Sorry, Rife, I had to do it."

"I know."

"Anyway, I squashed myself into a knife edge and I slashed through that air like my life depended on it. I didn't dare look back, because I knew it would slow me down. At around seven thousand feet I heard this bang, like a drum, and then everything went quiet. At one thousand feet I pulled out of the dive, slowly, because I knew if I didn't, at the speed I was going, I'd lose control. I literally, almost skipped off the ground, that's how long it took me to come to a more normal speed."

"And when you had slowed down enough to regain your bearings did you see Mr. Falco or his colleagues around?" asked Crow.

"No, that was the weird thing. I just don't know how they can clock me when I left them in my contrails."

Mr. Crow looked up from his scribbling and adjusted his monocle.

"They say here," he said, glancing at a very official looking paper he held in his one hand, "that they clocked you with ground radar."

"Oh, I guess that explains it. Because it was the next day they came and arrested me at home, in front of my parents. My mother was extremely upset and they were rough with me when they hauled me down to the station to take my photograph and fingerprints."

"Did they beat you?" asked Mr. Crow.

"No, but the one guy really wanted to, he kept trying to egg me on, saying 'one false move and I'm gonna knock some sense into you punk'. They just really pushed me around and jostled me more than was necessary."

"And then you were released into the care and custody of your parents, correct?" asked Mr. Crow.

Mallard nodded.

"I want to know why I wasn't charged too?" said Rifleman.

Crow put the papers on his lap and looked up at Rifleman through his monocle. His one bulging eye swimming behind that monocle like a fish in a bowl.

"I honestly don't know why," said Mr. Crow. "I

think perhaps they either didn't see you on the back of Mr. Mallard or they determined that you weren't an official party to the crime even if they did see you."

"But couldn't they have charged me with conspiring to commit a crime?"

"Well, yes, but that is a much harder crime to prosecute than actually finding someone committing the actual crime like they did here. I think that Mr. Falco and company didn't want to be bothered with the extra paperwork, considering they had a clear and egregious infraction right in front of them. However, I will be calling you to give testimony on Mr. Mallard's behalf."

Rifleman nodded eagerly.

"Do you think that's wise?" asked Mallard.

"I do. If we're going to try and get the judges onto our side we need to create a sympathetic story. I think telling them that you went up there to offer your friend a view of the world might buy us some sympathy."

"But what if they decide to charge him then too?"

Mr. Crow looked at his watch.

"What date is it today?"

"Twenty third of September," said Rifleman.

"Right, then you can't be charged with conspiracy because it is six months since the crime was committed. So no, Mr. Mallard, Rifleman will be safe from the possibility of charges."

"Whew," said Rifleman, wiping his brow with his hand in jest. "I'd give testimony any way for my friend."

Mallard patted him on the back.

"And I wouldn't let you if you could still be charged."

"Would you two like a private moment," said Mr. Crow, grinning at them.

"No," said Rifleman, laughing. "I was just saying, that's all."

"Good, because it's getting late and I want to quickly run over what you might expect at court tomorrow. You both haven't been at court before, right?"

Rifleman and Mallard nodded.

"Okay, good, that'll work in our favor. Now, most times, these sorts of trials can take days, sometimes even weeks. However, lately, Parliament has been rushing through these things, and not for the benefit of the accused I might add. And I fear that this might be one of those cases that gets rushed. In any event, there are only three main witnesses that the prosecutor will bring to testify."

"Who's that?" asked Rifleman.

"Well, firstly he'll bring forward Mr. Falco and his kin to testify to what they saw, thus setting the groundwork for why you were actually charged and what you were charged with. This is important, and I might try and pick at any holes that Mr. Falco's testimony opens up."

"What about the radar operator?" asked Mallard.

"That'll be part of Mr. Falco's testimony. He'll testify to both charges under Flying Without

Proper Featherability, section one hundred and one point two which relates to exceeding your altitude limit and then section one hundred and three point thirteen which is used to charge you with exceeding your speed limit."

"Who will the prosecutor bring up after Mr. Falco?" asked Rifleman

"My guess will be Mr. Rüppel. He'll need Mr. Rüppel's testimony to strengthen Mr. Falco's. Additionally, if you are correct, which I suspect you are, then Mr. Rüppel called the police on you and he'll need to testify to that."

"Aren't you supposed to get that information with all the other disclosures?" asked Mallard.

"I see you've been doing your homework, Mr. Mallard. Yes, I am supposed to receive the call logs amongst other things. But what I'm supposed to receive and what I've been getting from the court clerk's office have, lately, been very different things. I believe it's not by accident that they're limiting disclosure and my appeals have gone unanswered."

"Shit," mumbled Mallard.

"I feel the same way, Mr. Mallard, I do. But we have to work within the confines set up before us, to get you free, or at least punished by something other than clipping so that the work of the Congregation can continue."

Mallard sighed and looked down at his feet. He didn't like how things were going, and there was nothing he could do. He had to trust Mr. Crow.

"After Mr. Rüppel, I'd guess that the crown will call Dr. Branta Canadensis as you mentioned that he saw you at, what was it, twenty five thousand feet?"

"Yes," answered Mallard.

"I'm not sure how Dr. Canadensis will help the crown's case other than give additional credence to the fact that indeed, you were flying above your legal altitude limit. The key chink in the crown's armor as I see it, is that Mr. Falco is going to say you were flying at thirty three thousand feet like you told me, but they only caught up with you at, was it twenty three thousand feet?"

Mallard nodded.

"That's about where I believe we were at."

"Right, so I'm going to argue, even though it might be splitting hairs, that the charges are inaccurate because nobody saw you and can give evidence to the fact that you were at thirty three thousand feet, and as such, the charges should be withdrawn. Now, I don't believe that will happen, but it might give us a bargaining chip. At the end of the day you were clearly seen, by at least three witnesses, to be flying higher than your allowed limit of just under twenty thousand feet."

"I still think it's a ridiculous charge," said Mallard.

"And I agree, but we're playing in Parliament's nest now, so we have to use their rules to limit the damage."

Mallard twiddled his thumbs in his lap as he stared off at a distant point somewhere in front of Mr. Crow's feet.

"I'm just wondering how they figured out we were so high up. I mean, maybe they know something we don't?" said Rifleman.

Mr. Crow shuffled the papers in his lap and looked down at one in particular.

"I think we'll find that out tomorrow, they definitely have you down here with being charged at that altitude, and being above thirty thousand feet carries additional penalties as you probably know."

Mallard shook his head.

"No I didn't know."

"Well it does. Twenty thousand and above, in your case as a duck, is where the charges start. Above twenty five thousand and there are increased penalties and above thirty thousand is where the severest penalties are."

"So how do you think they might have figured we were at that height?" asked Rifleman again.

"If I was to guess, I think Mr. Rüppel probably saw you much earlier than you saw him, and being an expert at those altitudes he likely told Mr. Falco and comapny what altitude you were flying at. However, he is not an agent of Parliament and as such, you can't be charged based solely on his testimony. It's sloppy police work."

"But this whole thing is sloppy. The way society is going, the way you say Parliament is gunning for more authoritarian power. The whole thing is sloppy and stinky."

"I know, and we'll change it soon enough through the Congregation, but our immediate concern is tomorrow and your trial. And that, Mr. Mallard, requires that we work within the system for now."

Mallard didn't say anything, he continued to twiddle his thumbs.

"What happens after the prosecutor has brought all his witnesses forward?" asked Rifleman.

"Well, I'll get to cross examine them and then I'll get a chance to put the two of you on the stand. And this is where you need to show some remorse, make it how you just wanted to take your little friend up for a view of the world. Promise never to do anything like this again, and ask the court for leniency. If all goes well, then we shouldn't have to worry about your wings getting clipped."

"And me, what should I say?" asked Rifleman.

"Basically the same things as what Mr. Mallard attests to. You're just going to back him up, how you were just so excited to see the world from on high and you didn't mean any harm by it. And you'll also ask the courts for leniency on behalf of your friend. Any questions."

Mr. Crow took his monocle off and looked at the two of them. Rifleman shook his head. He was nervous, but he'd do the best to help out his friend. Mallard still stared down at the floor and slowly shook his head too.

"Good, I'll be there to help coach you through it. My questions will lead you to the right answers. Now, there is one last thing."

"What's that?" asked Mallard, sighing like a big deflating balloon.

"Well, the prosecutor will get to ask you some questions after I'm finished. I'll object as much as I can, but what you two must do, is not to offer any information that isn't asked. Keep it to simple yeses and nos if you can. If you can't, keep your answers as short as possible. Be polite but be brief."

Rifleman nodded.

"I understand, Mr. Crow. I sure hope this will work for Mal."

"I believe it's our best chance."

Mr. Crow looked across the room and out the window. The sun was just a dark red sliver of a frown on the horizon.

"It's getting late, you young men should be getting home."

Rifleman jumped off his chair and stood up, waiting for Mallard. Slowly, Mallard stood up from his chair as if he were wearing a leaden suit. Mr. Crow held out his hand and they both shook it. They followed Mr. Crow to the door which he opened for them and led them out.

"Go straight home now, there's a lot of talk about this trial on the streets and you don't want to invite any trouble before the trial starts. Okay?"

Mr. Crow tried his hardest to look at them sternly. But it was difficult, he had a soft spot for this pair of unlikely friends. As for Mallard, well, he reminded him very much of the Legend of Blackened Blade, and he might yet become the hero of change, if they could get through tomorrow. And who would've thought that a duck, of all birds, a waddling duck, could ever possibly lead them to a brighter future. Mr. Crow smiled at the thought. It would be one for the history books alright.

"I'll be sure to take Mal straight home, Mr. Crow, you can count on me."

Mr. Crow leaned down and patted Rifleman's small head.

"I have no doubt," he said.

And with that he watched them fly away from his office in the gnarled oak tree. He watched them for a moment. A curious site, the big duck like a large plane being escorted by a small fighter jet. Then he walked back into his office and started planning out his arguments for the next day.

Mallard and Rifleman weren't far from Rifleman's home when they were ambushed by Mr. Nestor Notabilis and three of his friends. They jostled and buffeted them in the sky, slowly bringing Rifleman and Mallard down to the ground, just off to the one side of Squire's Spoon.

Mallard landed first and Rifleman just off to his side. Mallard put his arm out and took Rifleman under his wings. The Kea led by Mr. Notabilis encircled them and closed in on them threateningly.

"What the hell are you doing?" asked Mallard, a mixture of fear and anger, spicy in his voice.

"We've come to offer you a warning, duckwad," said Nestor. "Don't try anything funny tomorrow alright, or you'll be sorry. I'm sick of your kind trying to be better than you are. You're nothing but a duck and that's all you are. You need to learn your place. You take your punishment and you repent. You're not better than us."

"I'm not trying to be better than you," said Mallard, "I'm just trying to be better than I am."

"It's the same thing," said Nestor, poking Mallard on the chest with his finger. "You shouldn't be encouraging others to stretch beyond their Zhengi given place in Broken Beak Woods."

"Stop poking me."

Mallard gritted his teeth, but Nestor kept poking him.

"I said stop it!"

"Or what. You're gonna quack all the way home to mommy," said Nestor.

Nestor's friends started laughing. Mallard got mad and his blood bubbled and boiled. He clenched his fist and as Nestor was looking at his friends, laughing along with them, his finger still poking Mallard on the chest, Mallard swung his fist right into Nestor's mouth. Nestor staggered backwards trying to keep his balance.

Nestor's friends came fast on Mallard and knocked him to the ground. Rifleman flew up and tried to dive bomb them away. One of them knocked him to the ground where he skipped along like a pebble on the grass before hitting his head on a rock and becoming unconscious.

Nestor got up and wiped the blood of his lips and walked back up to Mallard.

"You shouldn't have done that duckwad. Hold him down!"

And Nestor's friends held Mallard down, pinned his wings to the ground and Nestor kicked him in the side and punched his face.

"I should kill you myself, but I'd rather see you starve or be pecked to death by the predators when your wings are clipped. You're too big for your wingspan, duckwad. You remember what I said. We don't need no heroes and if you ever try to become more than you think you are, we'll be more than willing to cut you back down to size."

And with that, Nestor kicked Mallard one last time in the face, his claws slashing him open across his left eye and cheek. It would leave him with a scar but it wouldn't cost him his eyesight.

"You've been warned duckwad. This is your only warning."

And as quick as Mr. Notabilis and his friends

had come, they left. Mallard got up and rubbed the side of his stomach and gently touched his face. His fingers came back bloody and he winced.

"Rife!" he yelled, "Rifleman, where are you?"

He got up and looked around, and then he saw Rifleman with his head at an unnatural angle by a rock. He waddled up to him as quick as he could. Mallard leaned down and picked up his small friend.

"No! Rifleman, what have they done to you."

Mallard cried and held his friend to his chest as he picked him up and flew them to Dr. Canadensis clinic. Halfway there Rifleman recovered consciousness.

"Why the tears?" he asked.

Mallard looked down and grinned. He wiped them away.

"I thought you were dead, Rife."

"It'll take a lot more than a couple of Kea to do the Rifleman in, though you look like you've seen better days."

"We both have," said Mallard, "I'm taking us to

the clinic. I'm so sorry I got you into this, Rife. I really am."

"I wouldn't have it any other way."

Parliament

It started early in the morning. The sun had wobbled out of bed and was just now steadying itself on its feet. Mr. Crow was waiting outside Parliament for Mallard and Rifleman. They were running late, and the court hated tardiness. Mr. Crow glanced at his watch again. He'd been given five minutes to find the two of them or they'd be tried and no doubt found guilty in abstentia. That fair principle of natural justice, audi alteram partem had lost favor for some time now at Parliament and proceedings against those charged with crimes were commonly being carried out without their or in many cases even their lawyer's presence.

There were two minutes left when he thought he saw what looked like Rifleman and Mallard far on the horizon coming towards him. Mr. Crow took to the air flying awkwardly with his broken wing towards them. He was going to give them a piece of his mind about their lateness, but as he caught up with them, he understood why.

"Good Zhengi, what happened to the two of you?" asked Mr. Crow.

"Nestor Notabilis and his Kean friends caught up with us last night," said Rifleman.

"We'll have to report this," said Mr. Crow.

"We already spoke to Mr. Falco and his friends last night at Dr. Canadensis' clinic. They didn't seem all that concerned," said Mallard, "in fact, he just took down some notes and said he'd look into it. But he won't. He was just going through the motions."

"Are you okay, though?" asked Mr. Crow.

"Yeah, I got thirteen stitches for this gash and I'm banged up, but Rifleman just got out, he's been under observation the whole night. The Keans kicked him into a rock and he took a pretty bad concussion."

Mr. Crow looked at Rifleman, he looked, from the outside to be in better shape than Mallard. Though as he looked closer, he saw his knitted scalp and the clotting blood at the back of his head.

"Have you been given the all clear to be here today?"

Rifleman nodded and then chuckled, which made him wince, his skin pulling at the back of his scalp.

"You should have seen the other guy," he said. "Not a scratch on him."

Mallard laughed aloud, Mr. Crow smiled discreetly.

"But have you been discharged from Dr. Canadensis' clinic?" asked Mr. Crow again.

Rifleman and Mallard looked at each other, guilty smiles on their faces.

"Not exactly," said Rifleman, "but honestly, Mr. Crow, I feel terrific."

Mr. Crow looked at them steadily, before nodding somberly.

"Okay, I won't argue with you, because we don't have the time, they're going to start without us any minute. Let's get to it."

The three of them arrived in the courtroom just moments before the three judges walked in. They all stood until the last of the judges had sat down. In the middle was Tyto Alba. To his left was Asio Otus and to Tyto's right was Bubo Africanis. It all looked very official and the judges with their red and black robes and white wigs of feathers gave the whole affair an air of dignified order.

Accipiter Striatus and colleagues, Mallard counted five of them, were positioned around the court. These hawks were court security, and two of them were placed on either side of the judges high bench. Another two were at the back of the courtroom guarding the entrance, and the fifth was off to the left of Mallard, keeping a steely eye on him.

Mallard looked past Mr. Crow who was on his

right and at the prosecutor. The prosecutor was a very well dressed, dignified man by the name of Mr. Jubula Lettii. He was smartly dressed in a brown suit and his tuft eyebrows gave him a very dignified and wizened look. Mr. Crow looked downright schlumpy in comparison.

"We are here today regarding the matter of Mr. Anas Platyrhynchos v. Crown, in the manner of Unlawful Flight, specifically Flying Without Proper Featherability, sections one oh one point two and one oh three point thirteen. What say you Mr. Lettii?" asked Tyto.

"I say same my Lord."

"What say you, Mr. Crow?"

Mr. Crow stood up and looked down at the desk in front of him. He shuffled some papers around until he got the one he was looking for. He took a moment to look at it.

"Mr. Crow?"

"Ah...yes, my Lord. I say same."

Tyto Alba looked down at Mallard from up on his high perch. Mallard couldn't remember the last time anyone had used his official name.

"Parliament is delighted that you decided to join us Mr. Platyrhynchos."

"I...er...I got held up..."

Mr. Crow put his hand across Mallard's mouth, turned to him and whispered into his ear.

"Don't speak to the court unless you are asked a question."

Mallard looked down at his lap and tapped his fingers on his legs.

"Is your client aware of court protocol, Mr. Crow?" asked Asio.

"Um...he is a quick study my Lord, he is now aware."

"Very well, let us proceed," said Tyto. "I'll take opening statements from Mr. Lettii for the crown first."

Mr. Lettii stood up but he didn't say anything. Tyto looked down at some paper on his desk and picked up his gavel.

"Please proceed, Mr. Lettii," said Tyto slamming down the gavel.

Mallard jumped. His trial was underway. There were very few people in the back benches watching the proceedings. Mallard didn't think this was a good sign. If the people weren't interested in the law and justice, how would the Congregation ever get them interested in a revolution. He turned his head to look behind him. Rifleman was in the first row of seats, listening intently to the goings on. To his left was Ms. Pica with a briefcase that seemed to be bulging at its seams.

The back row seemed to have a few members of the press present, including one man who was nodding off with his hands folded in front of him and his fedora bobbing up and down like a sea buoy. Other than that, an assortment of birds, Mallard counted seven, were scattered about, paying scant attention to his trial.

"...that is what the accused is charged with."

Mallard brought his attention to the front and started to listen to the prosecutor.

"I know there are some of us here who feel that these charges are at best minor nuisances. But

I urge Parliament to take a hard stand on the egregious and flagrant disregard that the accused shows for our laws. Mr. Platyrhynchos thinks nothing of thumbing his nose at Parliament, and indeed, society at large with his incredibly reckless behavior. If we do not clip his wings, if we do not make an example out of him, it won't be long before he ends up murdering someone. This is the slippery slope of arrogance that the accused is about to embark upon. There are reasons why we must limit our potential for the better good of the flock at large..."

Mallard had to agree that the prosecutor was good. He even started to feel a little guilty for what he had done. And all he had done was try and stretch his wings a bit, fly out of his comfort zone. Nobody was hurt, not even close, and the potential to benefit society, or the flock at large as he said, could be incalculable if all birds were allowed to pursue the passions in their souls. Yet, as he sat there, listening to Mr. Lettii, Mallard felt small and scolded, as if he had just been found red handed with a knife in his hand, standing over an innocent victim.

"The crown will show Parliament how the accused flagrantly disobeyed known laws and put the flock and his small friend at great risk. For that, he must receive the harshest punishment. Thank you my Lords."

Mr. Lettii sat down, shuffled his papers together in a neat square and then put them neatly back down on his desk.

"Very erudite. Very well constructed argument Mr. Lettii," said Tyto.

Mallard thought he could see a smile at the corners of Mr. Lettii's mouth. He also didn't think it was very objective for Parliament to be making such nice comments about the prosecutor's statements.

"Why did he just congratulate him on making such a good argument. I thought Parliament was supposed to be impartial," Mallard whispered to Mr. Crow.

Mr. Crow leaned in towards Mallard.

"Let's not worry about that right now. I have to make opening statements."

"Mr. Crow, it pleases the court to invite you to make open statements. Please keep it brief," said Tyto.

Mr. Crow stood up and waited for Tyto Alba to slam his gavel down which he did.

"It is a privilege to be here before your Lordships, I only wish it were under better circumstances..."

"Get to the point, Mr. Crow, we don't have all day," said Bubo Africanis.

"Yes, very well. Defense will not argue that my client is innocent. But rather that he made a mistake as many of us have done under the naïve enthusiasm of youth. My client is willing to admit his mistake and throw himself at the mercy of this gentle court..."

"Thank you Mr. Crow," said Tyto.

"But my Lord, I am not finished..."

"You are finished, Mr. Crow. Please be seated."

Mr. Crow sat down slowly.

"If you would call your first witness, Mr. Lettii," said Tyto.

Mr. Lettii stood up.

"Crown calls for Mr. Falco."

Mr. Falco came in from an adjoining room and took a seat on the stand. Mallard leaned in to Crow.

"This is not going very well is it?"

"No, son, I'm afraid it's not. I've never before been dismissed during my opening remarks. But keep the faith, I have some questions to ask Mr. Falco that could help us."

"Mr. Falco, you are the officer of Parliament who charged the accused with Flying Without Proper Featherability is that correct?"

"Yes it is."

"Could you tell us how you came to learn of the accused's egregious disrespect for our laws."

"My Lord, I must object to the hyperbole and leading tone of the crown's questioning. Nowhere in the regulations does it speak of the breaking of these laws as egregious."

"Overruled."

Mr. Crow sat back down and sighed. This was becoming nothing more than the facade of justice. A kangaroo court, the likes of which he thought he'd never see in his lifetime.

"I agree that the accused was egregiously breaking the law. The admirable citizen Mr. Rüppel brought this dangerous activity to our attention. We caught up with Mr. Platyrhynchos as fast as we could. Even at that time he was at twenty three thousand feet."

"Twenty three thousand feet!" said Mr. Lettii. "Well, I never. Are you sure?"

Mr. Falco nodded like a proud puffed up penguin.

"I most certainly am, I have all the records to back it up. But even worse than that, the accused was seen flying at thirty three thousand feet."

Mr. Lettii shook his head.

"You can't be serious, I thought that was impossible for a duck?"

"No sir, Mr. Rüppel saw it with his own eyes."

"Thirty three thousand feet. Is that not practically the limit to which any bird can fly?"

"Just about I believe."

"And the accused, a mere duck, had the audacity to flaunt our laws in such a heinous manner. Flying, I would like the court to note, at well over thirteen thousand feet higher than the already very generous limit allowed for his species."

"That's correct," said Mr. Falco.

"But that is just the beginning. Not content with breaking just one law, Mr. Platyrhynchos thought it fit to break others. Please tell the court what happened when you approached the accused."

"We reached the accused at twenty three thousand feet and identified ourselves as law enforcement. Flight at that height, even for trained officers like us, is extremely dangerous I would like the court to know."

"We are well aware of the risks that you and kin put up with every day to protect the flock. The crown and Parliament thanks you for this bravery and courage. Please continue."

Mr. Crow shook his head and stood up again.

"My Lords, I must protest. Can we please stick to the facts and not fawn over the witness."

"Overruled, Mr. Crow, this speaks right to the heart of the matter. The accused put not only himself and the flock at large in danger, but officers of the court as well," said Tyto.

"Well, like I said, at twenty three thousand feet we identified ourselves to Mr. Platyrhynchos as law enforcement."

"And what did he do then," said Mr. Lettii as he turned to look at Mallard, his tufts of eyebrows twitching like animated exclamation marks.

"He headed straight into a dive."

"He tried to elude the police?"

"Yes. We went after him but he kept gaining speed, at over two hundred miles an hour we had to give up the chase. He was simply putting too many members of the community at risk. In fact, he narrowly missed a flock of goslings' first flight."

"Do you mean to suggest that he was trying to frighten them, or worse?"

"I'd say he was at the very least trying to frighten them if not actually harm them."

"Heinous, I say, absolutely intolerable."

"I didn't do anything of the sort!" exclaimed Mallard.

Mr. Crow got up again. All this up and down was not as easy on his knees as it once had been.

"My Lords, I object strenuously. The crown is both leading his witness and allowing for hearsay and speculation."

"Overruled, Mr. Crow, and Parliament reminds you to watch your tone," said Tyto.

Mr. Crow sat down heavily. Never had he seen such abuse of the law and justice in all his many years of practicing, and he had practiced a long time, though his last case was over a year ago. He had heard from the Congregation that Parliament had changed drastically, but he could never have imagined this disgraceful subjectivity in all his years. He turned to Mallard. Mallard's eyes were wide as saucers and his jaw was slack.

"They're crucifying me. All this is just pretense. They're going to crucify me," said Mallard.

Crow put his hand on Mallard's shoulder.

"I know it doesn't look good. But we've got options, son. Just hold firm."

"Ground radar, clocked the accused at Mach 1.1 before he finally started to slow himself."

"And at what altitude did he finally come down to legal speed?" asked Mr. Lettii.

"He came under one hundred miles an hour at two hundred and seventy seven feet, again, putting many resting birds at risk as he brushed against some of the Redwoods' branches."

"I am astonished and appalled," said Mr. Lettii. "How did this make you feel?"

"Angry and indignant," said Mr. Falco. "Never before in all my years have I ever seen such flagrant disregard for our laws. I urge and beg the court to clip his wings so that nobody else might have their lives put in danger by this psychopath."

Up again, like a yoyo, stood Mr. Crow.

"My Lords, it is not within the jurisdiction of the witness to determine the sort of punishment fit for the crime."

"Sustained."

Mr. Crow sat back down. Finally, a small win, though the amount of leeway Parliament was allowing the crown was astonishing and depressing. Crow thought that the only solution was going to be his backup plan, and the revolution would have to be brought forward.

"I was just trying to see what I was capable of. I was only trying to pursue my Zhengi-given gifts to help others see what they were capable of!" exclaimed Mallard.

The gavel came down again and again, like a hammer upon steel.

"Silence!," said Tyto, "Silence!"

When Tyto had finished, in vain, trying to hammer a hole through his bench with the gavel, the court fell into silence. Mr. Crow had his hand on Mallard's shoulder squeezing it firmly. He was leaning in towards Mallard.

"Don't, son, you'll get into a heap of trouble."

Mallard's eyes were wet with tears. He was deeply injured by the injustice of this Parliament.

"Mr. Crow, another outburst from your client and the court will find him guilty of contempt. And you know the punishment for contempt, don't you Mr. Crow?"

"Yes, my Lord. Contempt carries with it mandatory clipping."

"Very well. That's your last warning," said Tyto, his face ruddy and wet from the effort and anger.

"All I was trying to do," mumbled Mallard, the words falling into his lap like broken glass, "was to try and better myself. To try and reach my limit and explore my potential."

"I know, son, I know. Let's just worry about getting through this. Please, let me handle any outbursts that might need to be made. Hold firm. You've done nothing wrong. In time, the flock will come to see your acts as acts of valor and bravery.

You'll be a hero, soon enough."

Mr. Crow patted Mallard on his back and looked back at the witness. Mr. Lettii turned and looked at Mr. Crow. His tufted eyebrows like menacing daggers. He then turned back around and addressed the judges.

"If it pleases my Lords, I now offer the witness to defense for cross examination."

"Very well," said Tyto. "Mr. Crow you may be proceed, with caution, I might add."

And he hammered his gavel down against the block. Mr. Crow stood up and slowly buttoned his black but somewhat frayed suit. He combed his hands through his graying hair and walked over towards the witness, Mr. Falco, stopping in the no man's land between them. He looked down, composed his thoughts before looking up at Mr. Falco. Mr. Falco's face was a solemn slab of grumpy granite.

"Were you the first on the scene?" asked Mr. Crow.

"I was," said Mr. Falco, "with three of my men

right behind me."

"And was my client injuring anyone or attempting to injure anyone?"

Mr. Lettii was up like a shot from his desk.

"My Lords, my most strenuous objection. The accused has not been charged with any crime of violence against any individual."

"Sustained," said Tyto. "You're on thin ice Mr. Crow."

Mr. Crow looked back behind him towards Mr. Lettii, he grimaced and took a deep breath. If he lost his cool, all hope for Mallard's lesser punishment would be torn asunder.

"Pardon me, my Lords. Mr. Falco, if I might retry the question. Did you see anyone else within a hundred feet of my client, other than his friend, Rifleman?"

"No, there were no other birds within one hundred feet of the accused."

"My Lords, I therefore request that Mr. Falco's previous statements regarding my client's wanton disregard of the law and that it put others at risk of injury be withdrawn. Clearly, with not other birds present within close proximity, it boggles the mind how Mr. Falco believes that my client could have had any intent to injure anyone."

Tyto leaned to his left and whispered with Asio Otus, and then he leaned to his right and whispered with Bubo Africanis.

"Parliament will allow Mr. Falco's previous statements to stand. We are satisfied with Mr. Falco's expertise as a witness and feel that his input into the danger posed by Mr. Platyrhynchos is well within his area of competence as an officer of the law. And as an aside, you'll refrain from snarky comments, Mr. Crow," said Tyto.

"I ask my Lords to strike Mr. Falco's comments relating to my client being mentally ill and a psychopath. Unless crown has not been forthcoming, I am not aware of Mr. Falco's credentials as a psychiatrist."

"Very well, Parliament will disregard any allegations relating to the accused's mental health. Carry on, please, Mr. Crow. The court grows tired of your grandstanding," said Tyto.

"Mr. Falco, you said that my client's infraction was brought to your attention by Mr. Rüppel. Is that correct?"

"It is."

"And based solely on Mr. Rüppel's word, you charged my client with an altitude of thirty three thousand feet, and yet you only saw my client at an altitude of twenty three thousand feet."

Mr. Lettii was up again.

"My Lords, I object to this line of questioning. Mr. Crow will have an opportunity to question Mr. Rüppel in good time."

"Sustained. Mr. Crow, this is your last warning, keep it civil."

Mallard was aghast. He couldn't believe how they were hamstringing Mr. Crow. He was neither being impolite or belligerent and he was certainly asking the right questions. Mallard looked at Mr. Crow, his feathers didn't seem ruffled. In fact he was incredibly composed considering the insults he was having to take.

"Mr. Falco, could you explain how you came to charge my client with an altitude of thirty three thousand feet when you only had visual verification of him at twenty three thousand feet?"

Mr. Falco, curled his lip into a snarl, maybe it was supposed to be a smirk but it was aggressive whatever it was.

"Mr. Rüppel called it in, and he gave an estimate of thirty three thousand feet. You're right, Mr. Crow, I saw the accused at twenty three thousand feet, but he got away from us. It was only the next day that we were able to arrest him and bring him down here to Yew where he was charged. Taking into account Mr. Rüppel's estimate, which turned out to be incredibly accurate, we charged your client based on the satellites that have been installed over the last year. We can see anybody doing anything at anytime."

Mr. Falco leaned back in his chair with his arms folded. Proud as a fat king on his throne looking over the bended backs of his thousands of slaves.

"Furthermore, Mr. Crow, these satellites are accurate within one foot."

There was an audible clamor in the courtroom from the few spectators who were there and the fewer who were actually paying attention. Mr. Crow's mouth slacked open for a moment before he caught himself. Never before had he heard of such flagrant abuse by Parliament of the flock's inherent right to privacy. Broken Beak Woods was indeed turning into a fascist dictatorship as he stood there in court watching like a helpless infant.

"My Lords, is this true?" asked Mr. Crow.

Tyto was banging his gavel, trying to bring order to the courtroom. The thing was, there wasn't much of a clamor. Not much noise that a few errant birds could make. When the courtroom was silenced enough to his satisfaction, Tyto turned to Mr. Crow.

"What Parliament deems necessary for the safety of the flock is none of your concern."

"But my Lord, this is a democracy, the people have a right to know!"

"You'll get your chance to be heard during the elections!" exclaimed Tyto.

"Which we haven't had in over nine years..."

"Enough!" yelled Tyto. "One more word, Mr. Crow and you and your client will both be in contempt. Not that it'll have much effect on you with your wing broken already as it is."

Mr. Crow bit his tongue and turned to look at Mr. Lettii. Mr. Lettii gave him a small shrug as if to say he didn't know about the spying, and that he didn't care either. He was emblematic of the problem that the Congregation was up against. Mr. Crow turned around and looked past Mallard and at the spectators. Such a sorry and sad bunch of birds he'd never seen, and these were the brave ones, the ones who might be inspired to fight for justice and equality and the ability to pursue one's Zhengi-given rights to be all a bird could be.

But the time would come when Mr. Lettii's use would come to an end, and the other intelligentsia and free thinkers would surely, come to see the tyranny for what it was. Even though it had started small, even a tyranny against one is a tyranny against them all. Mr. Crow sighed and looked up at the bench of judges.

"I have no more questions for this witness."

Crow went and sat down next to Mallard. He leaned into him.

"The revolution will have to be brought forward. Things are obviously much worse than I or the Congregation had expected."

"So this means I'm going to get clipped doesn't it?"

"Not if I can help it."

Mr. Lettii rose.

"If it pleases my Lords, I would like to invite Mr. Rüppel to the stand."

"Very well."

As Mr. Falco was leaving, Mr. Rüppel came in from the same side door and took his seat at the witness' bench. Crow only now realized that neither he nor Mr. Falco had been sworn in to tell the truth. Crow stood up.

"My Lords, I am just now aware that Parliament is not requiring witnesses to swear upon the Book of Beaks. How can we be assured of honest testimony?'

"You have not been at court for some time Mr. Crow. Parliament has seen fit to do away with childhood myths and fables relating to Zhengi. If you believe in fairy tales, you might be comforted by someone swearing on the greatest fairy tale of them all, that being the Book of Beaks. But Parliament has deemed the Book of Beaks and the belief in Zhengi to be incongruous with a society moving forward toward technology and science..."

"More like fascism and dictatorship," mumbled Mr. Crow.

"What was that Mr. Crow?" asked Tyto.

Crow looked up at the bench.

"If it pleases my Lords, I'd find great comfort in some reassurance that the witness' testimony will be the truth and nothing but the truth even if Zhengi will be of no help."

"Because the barrister is not up to speed with the new and streamlined court, we will indulge your request on this occasion."

Tyto Alba looked over at Mr. Rüppel.

"Mr. Rüppel, will you speak the truth today about all things?"

"Of course my Lord."

"Very well, the court apologizes to the crown for the theatrics, if you'll please proceed Mr. Lettii."

Mr. Lettii walked up towards the witness and stood leaning in on the witness box.

"Please tell Parliament what occurred on March eighteenth when you were flying on the day in question?"

"I was flying at twenty seven thousand feet, looking down for a place to picnic and find some lunch. I thought I saw something moving off to my right and above me. Nothing ever flies much higher than me except for other members of my kin and a few other species licensed to fly at thirty thousand, but this was a smaller thing. I looked up and saw a duck, can you believe that, a stupid duck of all birds flying up there at thirty three thousand feet."

"And do you see that duck here today in the courtroom."

"I do," said Mr. Rüppel, pointing his long hairy arm at Mallard.

"I ask the court to acknowledge that Mr. Rüppel is pointing to the accused, Mr. Platyrhynchos."

"So acknowledged," said Bubo.

Mr. Lettii turned back towards his witness.

"So what did you do?"

"Well, I feared for my safety, so I called the police right away. At first I thought that he had just been caught by a strong updraft, but then I heard him and his friend laughing and twirling and acting very dangerously up there. In fact, I heard him say he was going to dive bomb me. Obviously I got very scared."

"Thank you Mr. Rüppel, you did a great and brave service to the community."

Mr. Rüppel smiled and nodded his head, as chuffed as a cock alone amongst a brood of hens.

"I have no more questions, my Lords."

"Very well, Mr. Crow, you may question the witness, remembering that you are on a tightrope."

Mallard grabbed at Mr. Crow's arm.

"He's damn well lying, Mr. Crow, I never said anything about dive bombing him."

Crow turned to Mallard and smiled.

"I know, son, but it's going to be his word against ours, and we already know whose word the court prefers..."

"Mr. Crow!" exclaimed Tyto, "if you'll indulge the court."

Mr. Crow stood up and walked over towards the witness. He too leaned in on the witness box.

"Mr. Crow, give the witness some room, this is not an interrogation."

Crow stepped back several paces.

"Mr. Rüppel, would you have us honestly believe that a strapping specimen such as yourself, being twice as tall as my client, and weighing at least five times as much as my client, was scared of him?"

Mr. Lettii bounded up from behind his desk.

"My Lords, please, the barrister is badgering and argumentative."

"Sustained. Mr. Crow, you have now used up the court's indulgence with your theatrics, you many not ask anymore questions of the witness. The witness is excused."

Mr. Crow gritted his teeth. They might as well just clip his client now. This wasn't even pretending to be a just trial.

"My Lords, defense would like to reiterate its position that my client, Mr. Platyrhynchos is indeed deeply sorry for breaking the law and he throws himself at Parliament's mercy."

"So noted."

Mr. Lettii stood up.

"Do you have any more witnesses?" asked Tyto.

"I do my Lord. I wish to call Dr. Branta Canadensis to give testimony."

"Very well."

Tyto nodded to one of the court guards and he opened the door behind which, Mr. Rüppel had just moments ago disappeared. Dr. Branta Canadensis, dressed in the khaki and green of his profession waddled into the courtroom. He was dignified with a pencil thin moustache and wire rimmed glasses. His black hair was slicked back with gel and looked wet. He took a seat in the witness box.

Mr. Crow stood up, but Tyto waved him down bruskly.

"I know what you want Mr. Crow," he turned to Dr. Canadensis. "Dr. Canadensis will you tell us the truth today about all things."

Dr. Canadensis looked up and nodded solemnly.

"I will."

"Thank you, doctor, Parliament apologizes for having brought you here away from your more important work."

Dr. Canadensis didn't say anything, he was

looking at Mr. Lettii.

"Please continue barrister," said Tyto.

Mr. Lettii got up and walked over towards the witness stand. He smiled and looked back at the mostly empty court for some while.

"Dr. Canadensis, as Parliament mentioned, we are deeply grateful to you for spending some time with us today on these lesser matters. We know you are very busy helping the sick and injured, but we believe it is because of delinquents like the accused that you are busier than you need to be. With your gracious testimony, we'll certainly be able to put an end to Mr. Platyrhynchos' dangerous flying..."

Mr. Crow stood up, he was feeling it in his knees. They creaked like the innards of an old pirate ship in stormy seas.

"My Lords, can you please request crown to start their questioning, I didn't think we were doing summations."

"Sit down Mr. Crow, this is the crown's witness and we'll indulge him."

Mr. Crow sat down. Mallard looked at him.

"This is all just perfunctory isn't it? I mean they're just trying to put lipstick on the cadaver of justice's face."

"Well, yes, I suppose you could put it that morbidly if you wanted."

Mr. Crow stared ahead, looking at Mr. Lettii, puffed up and proud of himself. Like a murderous matador cruelly circling the bleeding and dying bull.

"What are you going to do!"

Mallard's voice was hushed but indignant. Mr. Crow didn't look at him.

"I think we've already lost. I think we lost the moment we walked in here. When Parliament becomes too powerful they steal from the people and they lose touch with who gave them that power. We need Parliament to become again what it was created as, a servant of the people. We need to start over, clearly. Parliament, having disbanded Congress sometime ago has become a rabid, ravenous uncontrollable beast with a taste for the flesh of the flock. As such, the only solution is to put it down."

"That's easy for you to say, I'm the one about to be sent to have his wings clipped."

Mr. Crow looked over at Mallard then.

"No, son, you'll be the one to lead us on towards a more egalitarian and just future. Just have faith."

Mallard slumped back down into his chair. He began to wonder if this old man, wizened, some would say, was slowly losing his mind right in front of him. How on Broken Beak Woods Mallard would lead anyone, let alone himself, to the promised land when he was behind bars having his wings clipped was beyond him. And now that the outlook of that punishment was beginning to seem more and more like a promise, he got scared and his stomach turned and his innards felt weak and mushy, like maggots.

"...it's because of these wretched members of our flock that these serious measures must be taken for everyone's concern and safety..."

Mr. Lettii was droning on and on. Mr. Crow turned around and looked at a bird sitting in the back row, listening intently to the trial. She was taking notes and dressed in a beautiful blue dress with a blue scarf about her neck and over her head. Her features were delicate and elegant. Ms. Cyanocitta Cristata was her name. She looked up and saw Mr. Crow looking at her. He nodded at her. She got up and discreetly left the courtroom.

"...so my question to you doctor is, did you see the accused flying beyond his altitude allowance at twenty five thousand feet?"

Dr. Canadensis nodded.

"Yes, that sounds about right, I saw him and his little friend flying around at twenty five thousand feet, having the time of their lives."

Dr. Canadensis smiled at Mallard. A warm smile without any trace of malice.

"And did you fear for your safety doctor, and the safety of your family and friends as Mr. Rüppel feared for his safety from this madman, the accused?"

Dr. Canadensis furrowed his brow.

"Well...er, no, I didn't. He was just out having fun, I see no harm in that. He was also fifty or more feet away from me. No, I never felt concern for my or my children's safety."

Mallard smiled. Here was a small win.

"Permission to treat the witness as hostile my Lords."

Tyto nodded.

"You may."

"This is a small win," said Mallard, looking at Mr. Crow and grinning at him.

Mr. Crow stared straight ahead.

"It won't matter I'm afraid. I believe Parliament's mind is already made up."

"But I thought you said you've never lost a case?" asked Mallard.

"That's right I haven't. But I also haven't been in court for about a year and how can anyone win when you're up against a rigged Parliament."

Mallard slumped back into his chair and twiddled with his fingers. This was it then, the beginning of the end.

"Are you sure, doctor, that you didn't feel even the least bit of concern for your safety. After all, the accused was flying extremely dangerously well outside his area of expertise."

Dr. Canadensis shook his head slowly.

"I'm sorry, sir, I just didn't see it that way. They were two young lads just out having some fun. No harm was intended I'm sure."

Mr. Lettii, for the first time that day looked a little flustered and embarrassed.

"My Lords, I'd like Dr. Canadensis' last statement stricken from the records. He is not an expert at criminality or psychology and I believe he has erred in his opinion of the danger that the accused poses towards the flock."

"Agree," said Tyto.

"Listen, just a minute, barrister," said Dr. Canadensis, "those two young men were at my clinic the whole of last night because they had been threatened by a group of Keans, acting as I believe on orders from Parliament..."

"My Lords, will you please instruct the witness not to speculate."

"So instructed," said Tyto. "Doctor, you will answer the crown's question and that is all."

"But this is just a facade, a kangaroo court to hang two young men as examples..."

"Order! Order!" shouted Tyto slamming down his gavel as if he was trying to split the block in two.

"This is a travesty. We have nothing to fear from birds trying to reach their potential, to stretch themselves. It is our Zhengi-given right to uncover our destinies, not to be corralled like sheep into the pens that Parliament dictates for us..."

"That's enough! Guard, remove the witness," yelled Tyto.

Tyto was hammering away at his block, the thick harsh knock, marking time to Dr. Canadensis' remarks. The guard came up to him in the witness box and hauled him off and out.

"...you'll not stop us, not all of us. We will have

our right to freedom and the fulfillment of our potential..."

That was the last to be heard from Dr. Canadensis as the door slammed closed after him.

"I didn't know he was with the Congregation," said Mallard.

"Neither did I," said Mr. Crow, smiling for the first time that morning. "This is an extremely fortuitous sign. The Hollow Hunger of the last year has obviously started to turn public opinion away from Parliament, more so than perhaps I had realized. The revolution will becoming soon."

"Not soon enough for me," said Mallard.

"We'll see, son, we'll see."

"I humbly request, my Lords, that the court disregards that outburst from the witnesses. I'd also like to suggest that the court notes that Dr. Canadensis didn't quite seem like himself today and perhaps his outburst is due to the overwhelming amount of stress brought on by the additional workload caused by the accused and his criminal kind," said Mr. Lettii.

Mr. Crow stood up, quickly this time, to hell with his knees.

"My Lords, I must protest most extremely. This is nothing but pure speculation and fantasy from my learned friend, Mr. Lettii."

They were hardly friends, but sometimes it paid to use good trial protocol in getting where you wanted to go.

"Overruled, Mr. Crow. Please sit down," said Tyto, and then he looked over at Mr. Lettii. "Never a truer word have I heard so far during this most difficult trial. Parliament extends its gratitude to you, Mr. Lettii, a rare friend of the courts, for your tireless efforts and long hours put forth for truth and justice..."

Mr. Crow and Mallard both felt sick listening to those sickly sweet self- aggrandizing words from the judge. Mr. Crow had not sat down.

"I'd like to cross examine the last witness, Dr. Canadensis, as is my right my Lords," said Mr. Crow.

"Dr. Canadensis, as you can tell has been

relieved due to stress. Clearly he is not well. In any event, the court has heard enough. Parliament will now take a recess to review the proceedings and come back with our judgement."

"My Lords, I haven't had a chance to call any witnesses, what about closing statements, these are all my rights and..."

The gavel was hammering away again.

"Enough Mr. Crow! One more outburst and I'll have you escorted to cells, leaving your client without counsel," said Tyto.

Tyto Alba stood up as did Asio Otus and Bubo Africanis. Those who remained in the courtroom begrudgingly stood up as the judges left. Just about everyone except for Mallard. The only reason Mr. Crow stood, was because he had been standing already. He turned and motioned to Ms. Pica who came up to him.

"It has started, Ms. Pica, please go and make the preparations. Reach out to Ms. Cristata and ensure everything is ready on that end. We have no time to waste."

Mallard looked up at the two of them and watched Ms. Pica leave the courtroom.

"What was that about?" he asked.

"I can't tell you, not yet, Mr. Mallard. But all will be made apparent soon enough. Hold tight and keep the candle of faith burning brightly in your breast."

Just about everyone had left the courtroom by the time the judges came back in. Everyone except for Mr. Lettii, Mr. Crow and Mallard, as well as the five court security officers. And in the far back was that same bird who seemed to have been sleeping during the whole trial. His fedora still bobbing up and down as he slept.

"Please be seated," said Tyto as he sat down.

Mr. Lettii sat down. Mr. Crow and Mallard didn't move, as they had not been standing in any event. Tyto looked down at his bench and read over some papers before looking up. He clasped his hands in front of him like a large stone and he looked down at Mallard with furrowed and worried brows. His beak pinched and pointed, his voice just as sharp.

"Mr. Platyrhynchos, you are here because you have been charged with Flying Without Proper Featherability, sections one oh one point two and one oh three point thirteen."

Tyto turned and looked at each of his colleagues in turn. First at Asio Otus on his left and then at Bubo Africanis on his right.

"We are all both shocked and horrified at your abhorrent behavior and flagrant disregard for the law. It is because of members of our flock like you, that Parliament needs to continually strengthen and tighten the laws and punishments to keep the flock here on Broken Beak Woods safe. Never in my thirty years on the bench have I had the displeasure of being witness to such callous disregard for society's mores and rules. Your flagrant disregard for the law is beyond comprehension."

Mr. Crow looked over at Mr. Lettii, his face was somber but he thought he saw the small curl of a smirk on the corner of his mouth.

"You say," continued Tyto, "that you were just out there having fun, trying to stretch yourself and to become all that you're capable of. Let me tell you, Mr. Platyrhynchos, that Parliament and its laws are there for a reason. To keep order and safety amongst all members of society. You might think that there is no harm done by pursuing your passion and fulfilling your destiny, but the harm is insidious and it is virulent. If we allowed ducks to explore their 'eagleness' and eagles to explore their 'duckness' all hell would break loose and society would boil over into anarchy."

Mr. Crow had difficulty stifling a chuckle, so he coughed instead. Tyto looked at him through sharp slits and furrowed more.

"We have rules and laws for the good of all of us. To think that you could ever soar like an eagle or dive like a swallow is tantamount to treason. You, Mr. Platyrhynchos, are a duck and duck is all you shall remain. I shudder to think what would become of us if we allowed those who had a yearning for risking ridicule and poverty and injury just for a momentary glimpse of greatness to march onward. The risks are too great. You could have killed yourself, worse yet, you could have injured others. No, Mr. Platyrhynchos, we cannot allow for self-realization and the fulfillment of potentials because you or any others feel that is their Zhengi-given right. We are a society of law and order, and everyone, from the African Crake to the Zebra Dove must abide by those laws and fill their allotted position and not some cockamamie scheme they think they should be allowed to fulfill."

Mallard looked down at his hands, tapping his fingers together. This was such nonsense. He couldn't stand to listen to it. How anyone could think that limiting possibilities was for the betterment of the flock was beyond him.

It was only when the one or the few stretched themselves, imagined they could be more than they were, that society flourished and improved. At least that was his hope and belief. And even if he was wrong, where was the harm? Where was the harm in trying to become more than you were?

"As such, Parliament hereby orders your wings clipped at first light on the morrow."

Tyto's gavel came down for the last time with a forceful banging as if it were the last hit that forged the blade. Yet the blade of justice and revolution had not even begun to be sharpened. Tyto stood up with his colleagues and walked out of the courtroom at the same time that Mallard was being dragged from the court by two of the security officers. He looked back at Mr. Crow.

"Keep the courage, Mr. Mallard, tomorrow is a new day. I promise you that, tomorrow is a new day."

And then he was behind closed doors, Mr. Crow's face, just a vision, a ghostly image he was no longer sure of. And as they dragged him towards the cells, a tear fell from his eye. To have his life ruined, really, to be given a death sentence just for trying to stretch himself, to offer his gifts to the world.. The injustice of it all burned hot like acid in his throat and his ribs closed in on his soft, beating heart and he stared at the bars of the cells as they went by, until he was tossed into one by himself.

And as the guards closed the gate on him, the world closed in on him and he felt alone like he had never felt before. To put a bird in a cage, surely must put the sky all full of rage.

Gaol

The cell was uncomfortable and the noises foreign to Mallard. He didn't sleep well the whole night. All the cells were full, they were small and they contained two to the cage. Just after midnight they tossed in a drunk warbler, his name was Mr. Sibilatrix. He snored the whole night, sleeping like a log while Mallard tossed and turned.

The warbler as well as the trickling pipes kept him awake. The pipes were perhaps the worst. The noise was a constant ticking and tocking like the clipping clock counting down his last hours and then minutes of flying ability he had left.

He had tried to snatch handfuls of sleep but he

hadn't managed well at all. Just as he might find himself dozing off his mind went to the last time he had flown, which sadly, had been straight to Dr. Canadensis' clinic with Rifleman in his arms. At the time he hadn't enjoyed that flight, but oh, just to be able to feel the air, slippery, over his feathers and around his body.

To open his mouth as he dived from the heavens fast as he could and his cheeks fill with air like balloons. If only he could once again fly through the jet stream which so few birds had ever done. To feel the temperature variations of the air currents. Some like the warmth of his mother's hugs, others as cool and cold as the injustice that gripped him even now.

He'd sooner kill himself, lying like he was now waiting for dawn to break upon him and clip his wings like shards of glass. The problem with trying to end his own life was twofold. Firstly, he didn't have any tools that might help him achieve that goal. And the second was that even the feeblest murmur of hope still beat in his heart. A hope that was perhaps at best unrealistic, and at worst the insane rambling pleadings of a madman.

Nobody was coming for him. Nobody was going to rescue him. He had taken his chances, he had broken the law and been caught. And now here he was awaiting his punishment.

And the thing that really sticks in his craw was the stupidity of it all. Not his own stupidity, but the unjust and stupid laws that had brought him to this place. As the flock outside slumbered, in both the literal and physical sense, Mallard's life was as good as over. And for what, he'd only tried to fly higher, faster than his forebears. Was that really such a crime. Should it cost him his life that he wanted to improve his own position, seek out his talents and make the best use of them? To show others who thought ducks dumb, just what they were capable of?

And if he could achieve such greatness as a simple duck, imagine what the whole flock could achieve if they were allowed to fulfill their Zhengi-given abilities and risk failure for a chance, a fighting chance at greatness.

Broken Beak Woods could become a literal paradise for all of them. A place filled with wonder and joy and a deeper peace and serenity than they had ever known. If they'd just let go of the fear. And it was scary, to try new things, to dream of greater opportunities. You could fail, and that was a hard pill to swallow, but easier still, than never trying and living with the regret and wonder of what might have been, what could have been if you had only tried.

As the Japanese Pittas said, if you fall from the sky six times, get up and fly again seven. Failure was only a pebble along the journey to accomplishment. Without failure, the nests of the Weavers would never have been developed. Mallard heard once, that the original Weaver had to try one thousand knots before he could build a nest suitable for his wife.

And the knot is just the very beginning. After that he had to figure out how to weave a thousand blades of grass into his very fine and majestic looking home. And yet without failure, without one thousand attempts at making that first knot, the Weaver line would have died out.

How many souls are being lost by not being allowed to risk it all on dreams and brighter futures. Just because old men wearing wigs and trying to look dignified in Parliament were scared of the outcome of progress. And so, instead of moving towards an egalitarian flock here in Broken Beak Woods, they were turning towards rigidity. Instead of improving aves' condition by allowing for the ultimate individual pursuit of potential and freedom, the flock was turning towards fascism.

And they slumbered while this was happening right under their beaks. They slept on while even now the Hollow Hunger kept gnawing at their empty bellies and withered souls. Piece by piece they were dying from lives of desperation and they didn't even know it.

And the worst part was the sacrifice that Mallard was making. Hell, he had never wanted to be a hero. He just wanted to have some fun, see what he was capable of, explore his potential. For when he was taking risks, exploring and flying at the best of his talents and skills, he never felt so alive, he never felt so much joy.

Even during his failures, the scrapes and bruises he'd taken along the way, he kept on trying and he improved and found his success in time. And now he wore the battle scars of failure as old soldiers proudly wear their medals of valor.

But he hadn't wanted this. He hadn't wanted to pay the ultimate price. In less than an hour, he knew that all he had worked hard to achieve, he would be butchered and his flying days would be over. He would be given stumps where feathered wings had once tickled the blue face of the sky.

He would, for the remainder of his days, just waddle the ground and if he could find the courage, perhaps bob on Blind Beggar's Pond, until eventually a predator would put him out of his misery.

Oh how mean, how cruel this fate for one who

had only wished to achieve his own greatness, and took the risks to do so. How heartless a brutish world to allow such punishment for dreams and hopes.

Mallard sat on the edge of his bunk. He was on the top one, his cellmate, the warbler, snoring below him, oblivious to his suffering at the slings and arrows of such foul fortune. The night sky was quickly trying on his different coats for Mallard's punishment. From the blue coat of the navy to the blue coat of the federation, night had paused a moment in the coat of duke's blue.

Mallard looked out at the awakening morning and knew time was slipping through his feathers, faster than the air during a diving flight. He sighed and put his head in his hands and gave up. He put his trust in Zhengi, if there even was a Zhengi, and at this, his darkest moment he lost his faith, but he sent up a prayer anyway. Perhaps, like a smoke signal, someone, somewhere might see it.

Mallard was lost in thought when he was snatched from his melancholy by sounds off at the end of the cell block. He jumped off his bunk bed and went to the cell bars and tried to crane his head through to see. He couldn't see anything but he could hear a soft commotion.

He held his breath and listened, he heard the mumble of voices but he couldn't make them out. He watched and waited, and after a short time the solid metal door at the end of his row of cells opened and he saw, first one and then a second of the biggest Golden Eagles he had ever seen. They looked menacing as they walked down the hall towards his cell.

Mallard's first thought was that these two were here to escort him to the clinic for his clippings. But then he looked out at the night sky and it hadn't quite lightened to the Brandeis blue of day. His next thought was that maybe they had been allowed in to kill him. Make it easier for Parliament to have him out of the way.

But as they walked down the hall, a small, in comparison, blackbird edged around them from the back. Mallard knew that face all too well. It had been a face he had become intimately familiar with over the last few weeks.

"Mr. Crow," said Mallard, trying his best to keep the whisper quiet.

Crow came up to him and shook his hand through the bars.

"We don't have much time," he said. "This is Mr. Aquila Chrysaetos and his kin."

Mr. Chrysaetos nodded his head as he took some keys from his belt and flicked through them with thick hands stuck on the broadest shoulders Mallard had ever seen. His face seemed small on his large upper body. A block of sharp, rough granite, with a few scars that bore witness to rough living. Though his eyes were soft and kind.

Mr. Chrysaetos opened the cell while his colleague stood guard, his immense back to Mallard.

"We've got to get you out of here. We caught them unawares during the changing of the guard. But we don't have much time before they realize what's happened and send a cast of falcons after us," said Mr. Crow.

Rifleman came up to the bars, squeezing in between Mr. Crow and Mr. Chrysaetos.

"Good to see you old friend," said Mallard.

"You too, Mal. You know this is the beginning right?"

"The beginning of what?"

"The beginning of the revolution, son. I told you yesterday that tomorrow would be a new day. And it is. The Congregation is waiting to meet you so we can lead the march on Parliament. There are many more of us ready than I ever imagined," said Mr. Crow.

"We've gotta get out of here," said Mr. Chrysaetos.

Crow led Mallard out of the cell and turned to Mr. Chrysaetos.

"Free everyone you can. You've got two minutes."

Ms. Pica was there too and Ms. Cristata. Introductions as well as greetings were exchanged as they moved quickly down the hall and out of

Mallard's cell block and through another and then a third before they made their way out into the open square behind the courthouse and Parliament where, just yesterday, Mallard had been sentenced.

Others were out there hiding in the dark corners. The sun would be peeking its lazy eye above the horizon at any moment. As soon as the five of them made it out into the middle of the square, the other birds joined them. It was an egalitarian and democratic mix of sexes, species and the different races that made up the flock of Broken Beak Woods.

It seemed to Mallard that everyone from the Albatross to the Weaver was present. And seeing the Weaver there filled Mallard's heart with joy. Here he was amongst kin, if not his own kin, the broader kin, or kindred spirits. And he felt for the first time in what seemed like many long days that there was hope for the people of Broken Beak Woods, if only they could hold firm, reinstate Congress and bring Parliament back to the people.

"We've got company!" yelled Mr. Chrysaetos as he exited the doors and entered into the open square. "Go, go, go!"

It seemed like a powerful hose had been turned on, as Mallard looked at birds spraying out from the open doors with great excitement and speed. But it was not all positive, Mr. Falco and his cronies were flying out too, taking down whoever they could.

In the confusion, Mallard took to flight, not thinking for a moment where any of the others were. He just followed the general stream. He looked around him and saw Rifleman trying vainly to catch up. Mallard swept round and picked him up, narrowly ducking under the sharp talons of a falcon.

"Let's get the hell out of here, Rife!"

"Agreed."

Mallard looked up at the sky and saw Mr. Chrysaetos off in the distance, his mighty wings carving up the sky like scissors. Ms. Pica and Ms. Cristata were with him. Mallard flew onwards until he reached them. Birds were thick in the sky as the sun opened its eye upon the world.

"Where are we going?" asked Mallard as he came up, shoulder to shoulder with the Golden Eagle. Mr. Chrysaetos looked at him briefly and then looked back ahead.

"We're going to join the Congregation and make our march on Parliament," said the big man.

"Where's Mr. Crow?" asked Mallard.

Mallard looked around but in the confusion and rush, he had lost sight of the wizened old man.

"I don't know," said the eagle. "But he knew the risks."

Mallard saw Ms. Pica and flew up next to her. Rifleman was holding onto Mallard for dear life.

"Where's Mr. Crow? Have you seen him?" asked Mallard.

Ms. Pica looked at him sadly and slowly shook her head.

"Blackened Blade knew the risks. He gave me strict orders to carry on, to take you to the Congregation no matter what happened."

Mallard furrowed his brow and his beak went slack. He didn't understand for a moment.

"Wait. What? You mean Mr. Crow is Blackened Blade?"

Ms. Pica smiled sadly and nodded.

"We can't just leave him, he'll be cut to ribbons by the falcons. He's got a broken wing. We can't leave him out there alone."

"We can and we will," said the eagle. "Blackened Blade knew the sacrifices that must be made. He had his eyes wide open, and he made us promise, under any circumstances, not to come to his aid."

"Well, he didn't make me promise," said Mallard, and he veered off left, sharply, and started flying against the current of birds.

"Shit," said Mr. Chrysaetos.

That wasn't working very well, so he flew up a few hundred feet above the thick of it which gave him a better view.

"We can't let him go alone, he'll get killed," said Ms. Cristata.

"I know," said the eagle and he veered off right to try and catch Mallard.

At the very end of the flock in flight, Mallard saw Mr. Crow gamely trying his best to fly as fast as he could. But he was being left behind. His right broken wing, hindering more than helping, causing much drag on his flight.

The flock was quickly leaving Crow behind, but Mallard had never before seen such committed determination and gritty courage as he saw Mr. Crow's face, a mask of irresolute resolve, despite the obvious pain.

Gaining on him were two falcons, their talons outstretched, sharp and glinting like knives in the yawning daylight.

"Watch out Mr. Crow!" yelled Mallard.

But he was too far away for Mr. Crow to hear. The first falcon was on him, slashing him deeply across the back and his broken wing. Mallard watched as his black coat parted and his blood, red, streaked across his back like a sash. The second falcon managed to slash at his neck and face as Mr. Crow started tumbling, losing height and stability but gaining speed.

"Hold tight, Rife!" said Mallard.

He tucked his wings tight next to him like the pointed edge of a spear. He dived, the air brushing past him, whistling in his ears. The falcons had dived after Crow as Crow tumbled helplessly towards the ground as he had once before as Blackened Blade.

Just as the falcons were about to make ribbons of Mr. Crow, Mallard reached them, crashing into them at one helluva speed. They tumbled over and over, Mallard almost losing control. He quickly stabilized himself and looked up for Mr. Crow who was coming down upon him, too fast. Mallard angled into a dive.

"Watch out, Rife, I'm going to try and catch Mr. Crow."

Rifleman looked up as Crow hurtled towards them. He moved over Mallard's back towards the right side, just as Crow landed and bounced on Mallard's left shoulder. Rifleman heard Mallard grunt.

"Are you okay?"

Mallard didn't say anything for a moment, the wind knocked out from.

"Yes...okay...grab...Crow."

Rifleman reached out his small arm and grabbed Mr. Crow around the neck and pulled him across Mallard's back.

"Got him."

Mallard was still falling. It was a heavy load carrying both Rifleman and Mr. Crow. He didn't know how fast or how high he might get. But his immediate concern was the ground trying to leap up towards him like a barking dog.

A few dozen feet from the ground, flapping his wings madly, Mallard started to gain traction and a grip on the air. Slowly he started to climb back up and towards the flock, who were now specks in the eastern sky just above the yellowing sun.

Mallard looked over his shoulder and the falcons were coming back for him. He didn't know what to do. But what he did know was that he couldn't out fly a falcon, not with the weight of Mr. Crow on his back.

"They're coming," said Rifleman.

"I know, I can see."

Mallard tried his best to dart and dodge, but the falcon was on him as if were attached by a short string.

"I don't know what to do!" said Mallard.

"Surrender," said Rifleman, chuckling.

Mallard was looking for a place to hide, but where could he hide that a falcon couldn't. He was so stupid, but what could he do. He couldn't leave the old man behind. He gritted his teeth and flew onward, his heart bursting with the effort. Maybe the falcons would grow tired, maybe he'd escape. Naïve hope, he knew, but there was a chance.

In any event, if he died here, now, at least he was flying, he was a free man. If he was going to die now, he would die on his own terms, flying through Zhengi's sky like it should be, because it was his Zhengi-given right to fly and spread his wings, to seek his purpose and to pursue, to hell with the risks and consequences. Because it was good and right and it honored his soul and the greater community.

Mallard looked back, the falcon was practically upon him. He felt the warmth of his friend on his back and the heavier wet warmth of Mr. Crow. These were not burdens. These were his friends and it was his honor and privilege to have come back for them even if now it would cost all of them their lives. He had lived with purpose and he would die with purpose. It had never all been in vain.

Courage and honor were the foundation of a life well lived. Mallard took a deep breath and closed his eyes, waiting for the talons to rip into his drumming heart, and to feel his last, final fall into the arms of Broken Beak Woods.

But nothing happened, so he opened one eye. Still nothing, and then he saw a falcon being hurtled towards the earth, tumbling end over end, his body streaked with blood, his squawks getting softer and softer. Mallard didn't understand he looked up and saw Mr. Chrysaetos above him.

"You've got an ostrich sized bucket of courage," said Mr. Chrysaetos.

"Or I'm just insane," replied Mallard, smiling at the big man. "Thanks."

"You're welcome. Let me take Blackened Blade from you."

Mr. Chrysaetos reached down and tenderly plucked Mr. Crow from Mallard's back with his immense talons. Mallard looked off behind him, the last falcon was returning towards Parliament. The chase had been called off, but the war had just begun. They flew to a Congregation clinic where Dr. Canadensis rushed Mr. Crow into surgery. He came out just a few minutes later. His face was sad, his glasses almost fogging up.

"I'm sorry," said Dr. Canadensis, "there is nothing we can do for him. He wants to see you."

Mallard, Eagle, Rifleman, Ms. Pica and Ms. Cristata made their way to Mr. Crow's bedside. Mallard looked at the old man lying in bed. His breath was labored and he winced as he tried to lean up onto the pillow. Mallard's eyes burned and he cried.

"Why didn't you tell me you were Blackened Blade?" Mallard asked.

"That was a long time ago, son, and it wasn't important. I had started a new life. I had tried to free us from the tyranny but it hasn't happened."

"You should have called out," said Mallard, as he sobbed now, "we could have rescued you."

He put his head on the old man's shoulder.

"We could have rescued you."

"That was not the purpose, the purpose was to rescue you. You need to take the baton from me and lead the flock of Broken Beak Woods to freedom and democracy."

Mallard got up and looked at Blackened Blade through blood stained, wet eyes. He held his hand.

"I can't, I am just a simple duck," he said.

Mr. Crow winced and looked at him through his coal black eyes.

"You are not a simple duck, Mr. Mallard, you are a bird of greatness, a warrior soul and a freedom fighter. You are braver than you realize and kinder than you believe. You have it in you to lead us. To bring a brighter future to Broken Beak Woods."

Mr. Crow took a deep breath.

"Promise me. Promise me, son, that you'll fight on. We've just about won."

Mallard looked at the old man, the living legend of Blackened Blade and he swallowed hard and his throat burned and his heart was squeezed with a great heaviness.

"I will," he said and he nodded. "I will, if you'll just stay with me."

Blackened Blade's eyelids fluttered and he looked at Mallard.

"I cannot be with you, but you are surrounded by friends and kin of all kinds. I am going back to Zhengi now. My work is done. Yours has just begun, son. Courage, for today is the new day. The beginning of our future of greatness."

And Blackened Blade exhaled his last breath and Mallard cried. Ms. Pica came up and put her arm around him. Rifleman reached up and took his hand. Even the big man, the Golden Eagle, had wet eyes. And they stayed with Blackened Blade until Dr. Canadensis came back and covered him with a sheet.

"Your life will not have been in vain, Blackened Blade, I promise you that," whispered Mallard as he left with his friends to make funeral preparations and to meet with the Congregation.

JASON BLACKER

About Jason Blacker

Jason Blacker was born in Cape Town but spent most of his first 18 years in Johannesburg. When not grinding his fingers down to stubs at the keyboard he enjoys drinking tea, calisthenics and running. Currently he lives in Canada.

Under his own name he writes hard boiled as well as cozy mysteries, action adventure, thrillers, literary fiction and anything else that tickles his muse. Jason Blacker also writes poetry and daily haikus at his haiku blog.

You can find his haikus and other poetry at his website **www.haiqueue.com**.

To stay up to date and learn about new releases be sure to visit **www.jasonblacker.com**

where you can find more information about his writing and upcoming projects.

If you enjoy space opera in the tradition of Star Trek then take a look at Jason Blacker's pen name "Sylynt Storme". It is under the name Sylynt Storme where you can find both sci-fi and vampire fiction written by Jason Blacker.

"Star Sails" is the space opera series and "The Misgivings of the Vampire Lucius Lafayette" is his vampire series.